ERA OF THE ULTRAS

MATT BLAKE

MATTBLAKEAUTHOR.COM

If you want to be notified when Matt Blake's next novel is released, please sign up to his mailing list.

http://mattblakeauthor.com/newsletter

Your email address will never be shared and you can unsubscribe at any time.

[1]

1970

MICHAEL WILLIAMSON WATCHED with nervous anticipation as his beautiful creation finally came to life.

It was a Saturday night. He knew what normal forty-year-old men did on Saturday nights. They were at home with their families. Maybe they'd take their wives out to a nice romantic dinner, or perhaps they'd spend time watching a cheesy movie with their children. Saturday nights weren't a time for working. They were a time for leisure.

For Michael Williamson, what he was doing right now was leisure, in a sense.

Just not the conventional kind.

Outside, he knew it was cold and frosty. He knew there'd probably be a mass of snow waiting on the bonnet of his Ford Escort. Good job his car was white. Michael loved his Ford Escort, though. Everyone had one. He'd always struggled fitting in when he was younger, and in all honesty, well into his adult life that struggle had continued.

But now he had his Ford Escort, he was just one of the crowd. He was normal.

As long as nobody heard him singing along to pop radio while he was in there. His voice would be enough to ruin that idea of normality for anyone.

In front of him was a massive sheet of glass. The glass itself was expensive. More expensive than he could afford to put in his home, that was for sure. Totally destruction-proof, apparently. Michael couldn't believe there was such a thing. Glass was glass. Hit it with enough force, and it was bound to shatter at some stage, right?

But he didn't want to risk hitting it. He knew what was behind it. The power of his creation. His idea.

Project Beta.

He looked up at the man propped above the ground. His arms were wrapped in metal, as were his ankles. His eyes were sealed shut. He was completely naked, but the metal conveniently covered him in the sensitive places, which relieved Michael 'cause he didn't want to be looking at any naked man today.

Not that he even saw Project Beta as a man anymore.

Project Beta was something new entirely.

He listened to the gentle hum of this massive underground facility, which could've been anywhere in the world. It was relaxing, really. Way more relaxing than those tapes Moira used to listen to. He wondered if she still listened to those now he'd left her. He wondered whether he was the person who stressed her out all along. If he was the reason she always seemed so down in the dumps.

No. He couldn't believe that. They'd had a good thing, while it lasted.

Just his work became too important. Way too important.

It wasn't her. It was him.

He had bigger concerns.

Like creating the most important self-defense weapon in American history.

Whenever he considered the consequences and the reality of what he was doing, he couldn't help but taste vomit and feel his skin crawl. He was just a normal kid twenty-five years ago. A normal kid living in a world where the war had just ended. Only he went to sleep worrying every night about what the world would become if war arrived again. He'd seen what'd happened, behind the scenes, once he got into the government. He'd seen the arms races between the superpowers. He'd seen guns, then nukes, then... then other stuff. Experimental stuff.

And he was going to be at the forefront of that final experiment.

The last form of true defense.

A defense that nobody would mess with. Nobody.

He looked up at Project Beta, eyes closed, brown hair dangling down the front of his face, and for a moment he saw the man.

And then that vision disappeared when he heard the door to the left slide open.

He turned around, startled.

When he saw who was walking toward him, his stomach turned.

Samantha Harvey was tall, blonde, and gorgeous. She had legs to die for and a smile that could end wars. But Samantha Harvey was no dummy. Samantha Harvey was tough. And she could use that smile to get what she wanted.

The way she was smiling at Michael right now, making his heart melt... yeah. Michael was pretty darned sure Samantha Harvey wanted something.

"Michael," she said. She glanced up at Project Beta, barely acknowledging its presence. "I hear the project is going well."

"Very well," Michael said, eager for any excuse to gush over his creation. "Vitals are good. And Project Beta seems really responsive to the serum."

"The serum?"

Michael did his best to contain his groan. That was the problem with pen-pushers like Samantha. They were intelligent, sure, but they didn't really understand the intricacies of the operation. They didn't *get* the significance of what was being created right here in this lab. "The serum based on our discoveries. The ones that we've been testing on prisoners for—"

"Right, of course, the prisoners." Her interruption was jarring and irritating. She looked down at a piece of paper, studying it closely like there was something lengthy and detailed written on there. Then she lowered it, looked at Michael and smiled. "We need to talk about a failsafe."

Michael felt his skin crawl. The "F" word. The word he'd been trying to avoid, all this time. "Respectfully, I've weighed up the pros and cons of a failsafe—"

"If this... this *thing* you're creating does work, then theoretically it should be powerful. A kind of powerful we don't want to risk crossing."

"We won't have to cross it because it'll be working for us."

"And if it doesn't? If it goes rogue?"

"Then it goes rogue. The chances are highly unlikely. It's just as likely that if we create a failsafe, that failsafe gets into enemy hands and they use it to threaten us."

Samantha kept on beaming that smile at Michael. Her big blue eyes flickered. "There's no negotiating. We need to develop a failsafe or the entire project comes down."

Michael felt a wave of sickness hit him with Samantha's latest threat. Because that's what it was, no disguising it. It was a threat, pure and simple, designed to put the frighteners on him. "That's a pretty radical step to take."

"As is creating a weapon without any kind of off switch. It's just the responsible thing to do, Michael. And you're going to do it."

"And if I don't?"

For the first time in their exchange, Samantha's smile faltered. Her stare intensified. Then within a flash, it was back to normal again. "You will. You know we have your best interests at heart. If you comply."

She nodded at Michael, and she walked away, her heels clicking against the hard floor of the lab.

Michael stood in the silence. He listened to the gentle humming, feeling relaxation seeping into his tense body all over again. He looked up at Project Beta. He didn't want to create a failsafe. 'Cause a failsafe meant that the second his beautiful creations were born, already they were prisoners to humanity.

Michael didn't want them to be prisoners to humanity.

He wanted them to be something else entirely.

A new race.

A new breed.

A new species.

Heroes.

He sighed and walked over to the door. He put his finger on the light switch, not wanting to flick it off, not wanting to go away from this place.

But he had an idea.

He had a plan.

He would create a failsafe.

But he'd create something else, too.

And then he'd see how Samantha liked it.

He smiled, took a deep breath, and flicked the switch.

A YEAR LATER, Michael finished constructing his failsafe.

FORTY YEARS LATER, and over fifteen years since the ULTRAs became public knowledge... a glint of sunlight bounced against a perfectly shiny metal object that'd been buried in the earth for many, many years.

Until now.

2

So, sure, I'd had a few damn good reasons to be anxious over the past couple years of my life.

But for some reason, the nervous anticipation of my eighteenth birthday topped it all.

The afternoon sun shone down intensely on Staten Island. It was the end of summer, that time of year where all the tourists start flocking in their droves because they are convinced that "tourist season" is over, only to realize that they in themselves are a tourist season. Yeah. You know the type.

That said, they'd picked a pretty good month to head over to New York this year. August had been freakishly cloudy by NY standards. It was the first of September, and if the rest of the month followed in this fashion, it was gonna be a treat.

If only I could get out of celebrating my birthday.

I squinted down the street at my home. It was just up on the left. My street was quiet, fortunately. Most of Staten Island was, in truth. You got the occasional day-trippers who took the free ferry from Manhattan, but they mostly disappeared again almost immediately. Not exactly a ton of things here to stay for. All of the fun was across the water.

I listened to the warm breeze carry a plastic Coca-Cola bottle across the sidewalk and realized I was thirsty. Hopefully, I'd be able to just get into my home and have as much drink as I wanted in peace. I'd gone out early to Manhattan. Just a day trip by myself. I took a lot of day trips by myself these days. Wasn't a lot else I could do now I was not only powerless in the eyes of the world, but not at school or college either. The summer vacation was coming to a close, marking two years since... well, two years since my life changed for the first major time. A lot had happened since. Hell, the world had almost caved in on itself a couple times.

But those days were gone, now. They were just memories, and I was just a relic. A barely recognizable relic that people occasionally nodded and smiled at in the streets. Sometimes people asked me for a selfie, and whether I really was all out of powers, to which my response was always the same.

I'd taken early retirement. Involuntarily.

Some people laughed.

Most people frowned, perhaps baffled that I wasn't as smooth as the archetypal superhero should be.

I guess one thing ULTRAdom couldn't prepare you for were the social skills to carry with you in the real world.

I got closer to my house, my body tensing. I couldn't shake the feeling that Dad had organized something super embarrassing for my eighteenth birthday, especially after all the whispering and grinning he'd exchanged with Damon, Avi, Ellicia, and Cassie.

Oh, Damon. Yeah, I still saw Damon. He was still my best friend. Let's just address that right away. He screwed up. He... he got involved in something he shouldn't have and ended up absorbing a load of powers. He blamed himself for Daniel Septer—Nycto's—death.

But even his powers had faded now. He hadn't had long to play with them.

I wasn't sure how they'd gone. Wasn't sure how he'd just lost them. I'd heard a few more talks of powers just disappearing, so perhaps it wasn't too absurd to assume that some powers had a kind of expiry date on them. Annoying, sure. But just a part of this mad world we lived in now. People always used to say what a mad world it was back in the old days. If only they'd stuck around to witness the ginormous freak show that was the twenty-first century.

I reached into my pocket for my keys when I heard footsteps just outside my home.

When I looked around, I saw three kids. They were all younger than me, probably fourteen, fifteen. One of them was chubby, larger than life with noodly brown hair. On the other side, a lanky Asian guy. And at the front of the group, a short ginger dude, who was anything but a "dude" but let's be kind okay?

They stood there and stared at me for a few seconds. Ginger blushed a little, kept glancing up and down from the sidewalk.

"You guys okay?" I asked.

"Are you him?"

"Hmm?"

"Are you... are you really Glacies?"

I felt my face start to burn. My stomach sank. Fans. Just fans. Unthinking, I reached into my pocket for my pen. "I used to be Glacies. But—"

"We heard you used to get bullied," the big guy said. "At school. Any... any tips?"

I looked at these kids, and I felt pity for them. They weren't so different from how I used to be. In another life, this could've been me, Damon and Avi.

I cleared my throat and started signing the comic that the

lanky guy held out. "Just be yourselves. No matter what. Don't change for anyone."

"Easy for you to say."

"Huh?"

"You found abilities. Easy for you to say when you changed more than any of us."

I sensed some animosity in the ginger guy's voice, and I wasn't sure I liked it. So I handed him back his comic, smiled and turned away. To be honest, I didn't like encounters like this. I felt guilty. Guilty that I couldn't be the hero these people wanted me to be anymore.

And why not?

Ironically, because it was better that they saw me for what I once was. Not for who I was now.

It was better that my heroics were in the past so that the pressure and expectation weren't on for the future.

I shuffled over to my front door and unlocked it.

When I opened it, I was met by a beautiful sound. Silence.

I walked down the hallway, hearing my footsteps echo against the fresh wood that Dad recently put down. He fit furniture now. That's why I hadn't seen him already today. He started work real early and finished real late. I kind of liked the space of the place to myself.

I walked toward the kitchen, opened the door, bracing myself for some kind of grand welcome.

There was no one home.

"Not even a card?" I muttered. I didn't mean to be disappointed. I didn't want a fuss. But surely everyone hadn't just forgotten me, right? Surely everyone hadn't...

I saw the photograph of Mom on the mantelpiece. The one where she was cuddling Auntie Stef's Labrador, that infectious smile on her face. The smile *before* she thought Cassie was lost.

I wanted Mom to be here. Of anyone, I wanted to celebrate

my birthday with Mom. Sad, I know, but that was the truth. She was my real best friend. She was my—

I heard footsteps behind.

When I turned around, I heard the voices before I registered who they belonged to.

"Surprise!"

I saw the smiling faces of the people I knew, heard the party poppers, but my gut reaction made something spark across my hands. Something cold stretched across my palms, seeped up my forearms.

Damon.

Avi.

Ellicia.

Cassie.

Dad.

I saw their laughter, saw their smiles, and I composed myself.

I made the ice go away and tried to look happy.

But as they surrounded me, hugged me, wished me a happy birthday, I kept my palms covered completely.

I'd almost sparked my powers and given them away.

I couldn't give them away.

Because I had to keep everyone believing that I didn't have powers anymore.

I had to keep my abilities a secret because I wanted to live a normal life.

I had to keep them secret because I didn't want to be a hero anymore.

3

It turned out Dad didn't have anything too zany planned. Just a meal for family and friends at Pazza Notte over in Manhattan. I liked the place. They did delicious pizza. So I couldn't exactly complain.

Not until Cassie leaned over when I was halfway through my tiramisu and gave me a very silent lecture about responsibility, something she seemed to be making a hobby of lately.

"They're going to find out eventually," were her words. And as she spoke them into my ear, I knew exactly what she meant right away. See, I might be able to keep my powers from the world; I might be able to keep them from my friends. I might even be able to keep them from my dad, and from my girlfriend.

But there was no keeping anything from my sister.

God bless her.

God damn her.

"They won't find out."

"They will if you keep getting icy fingers every time you get a little bit scared."

"Look," I said, wincing as I hoped Cassie would keep her

voice down. "It's my birthday. My eighteenth. We don't have to talk about this here."

"Kyle, don't mess with me. You didn't even *want* an eighteenth."

"Definitely keep that quiet."

"I'm just saying we need to be more open. More honest."

"There's nothing stopping you being more open and honest. I've made my call."

"You know I'm not as strong as I was."

"That's not—"

"It is true. You know as well as I do that something happened in the fight with Adam. I'm weaker now. I can't just go representing this family alone."

"Then don't at all," I said, looking into her eyes. "We've done what we have to do. The world's okay now. Sure, there's more ULTRAs floating around. But crime's down. People are happy. Well, still miserable, but happier. Why can't you just accept that?"

Cassie sighed. She sipped back on her vodka cocktail, and then looked around the table. To her left, Avi, who I swore had a massive crush on her. Further around the table, Damon, Dad, Sarah—a woman who Dad insisted wasn't his girlfriend but who he seemed to be getting along awfully well with. And on my right, Ellicia.

Cassie leaned in again. "I just think it's about time you grow up. Take that whichever way you choose."

She leaned over to Avi then, who seemed massively grateful for the conversation.

I looked around the restaurant. Looked at the young people at the bar sipping their alcoholic drinks, some of them glancing over at me like I was some former reality TV star. I saw the older people looking at me with skepticism and cynicism between bites of complimentary bread. As much as I was trying to outrun what I truly was, I could still feel the draw of being an ULTRA—being Glacies—sinking its nails into me and holding on for dear life.

I knew it was bad that I wanted it to let go. I had powers. I should make the most of them. Enjoy the fact that I was special.

But I'd seen what being special did. I'd seen that being special didn't bring happiness. It didn't bring joy, at least not for long.

Being special only brought pain.

Mum was proof of that.

As was Orion.

As was Daniel. My brother.

Just thinking of them put me off finishing my tiramisu.

"You okay?"

I jolted back to the present. When I looked to my right, I saw Ellicia. She looked nice, her chocolate brown hair cut a little shorter than usual. She wasn't wearing her glasses, opting for contacts instead. She was staring not at me but at my tiramisu.

"I'm fine," I lied, feeling a little hot in the face. "Why?"

"You've been staring at that tiramisu for ten minutes without putting any of it in your mouth. Starting to think there's something seriously wrong."

"Oh," I said, scooping some of the sloppy tiramisu in, the alcohol-coffee kick making me cringe a little. "It's... I think the cream's off."

"The cream's not off. Mine was fine."

"Maybe you like off cream," I said, forcing it down my throat and almost choking in the process.

"Trust me," Ellicia said. "I don't."

I shrugged. I didn't know what else to say.

Then she opened her mouth and laughed. "You still have that thing?"

I looked at where she was looking and saw the little almond

necklace she'd goofily made me in her arts and crafts class just after we first met.

I scooped it up off the floor, where it'd dropped. "Course I do."

"Even though you're allergic to almonds?"

I smiled. "Couldn't bring myself to tell you that when you first made it me. And I guess I've just... held on to it since."

She smiled, her eyes flickering.

Then she reached over and grabbed my hand, totally out of the blue.

"Kyle, I'm going to USF."

If I had any tiramisu left in my mouth, I would've spat it out at that moment. "USF? I thought you were going to Yale."

"I've been thinking. About what I want to do. About my future. And USF has the best marine biology course. And there's a place available there. Last minute, but—"

"Marine biology? I thought—"

"Aren't you happy for me?"

I wiped the corners of my mouth. My heart pounded. The laughter, the heat, everything in this restaurant suddenly seemed dialed up to a million. "Of course I'm *happy*."

"You don't seem happy."

"I am. Honestly. It's just... I wasn't expecting it. That's all."

"You know, you should think about applying, too."

I frowned. "To USF? You think they'll take a guy like me who hasn't even finished school, technically?"

"You had ULTRA things to attend to. They'll understand. Besides, a friend I've been talking to there. One of the lecturers. He says he's looking to hire someone big from the ULTRA world. Launch the world's first ULTRA Studies course. I think you'd be perfect for it."

I felt a mixture of emotions at Ellicia's revelation that not only had she been chatting to a lecturer from USF, and not only was he male, but he wanted to hire me to lead a class that looked into ULTRAs. "I..."

"Just think," Ellicia said, shuffling closer to me. "It'll be great. You and me, at college together. You there as a lecturer, me there as a student."

"There're rules against that, you know?"

She punched my arm playfully, then scooped some of that leftover tiramisu into her mouth. "What do you say? Teacher?"

I wanted to keep this going between us. But in the end, I could only sigh, unable to hide my fear or disappointment or whatever it was.

Ellicia clearly saw my reaction. She put the spoon back into my bowl. "That's a no, then?"

"It's not a no. It's just—"

"I'm sick and tired of you making excuses," she said. "You don't want me to leave New York. You don't want to leave New York with me. You don't want to do *anything*. Just sit around and mope. Well, I'm sorry. I'm sorry that you happened to get a load of powers just before we finished school then lost them all over again. I'm sorry you want to stay standing still and don't want to grow up. But that's not me. That's not who I am."

I felt my hands getting colder. When I glanced to my left, I saw Cassie looking at them as they rested on my knees. She knew. She knew exactly what was happening. Nobody else did, but she did.

Part of me wanted to just be straight with Ellicia. Tell her the truth. Tell her everything about my powers, and why I'd kept quiet that I'd got them back.

But I knew how she'd react. I knew she'd go back to begging me to take responsibility, and things like that.

I was done with responsibility.

I was done with Glacies.

I just wanted to be Kyle Peters again.

"You need to grow up," Ellicia said, dabbing at her eyes. "Before the world grows up around you and leaves you standing still."

I opened my mouth to respond. To ask her to clarify what she was saying.

And then I heard gunfire outside the restaurant, followed by a blood-curdling scream.

4

I heard the gunfire outside Pazza Notte, and I felt my hands getting colder than they'd been in a long while.

The restaurant went silent. Everyone at my table and every other table turned around, immediately stopping what they were doing for a look outside the window. The gentle background music of acoustic guitars continued to play, creepy amidst the rest of the silence.

"There's... there's somethin' goin' on," a guy in a suit to our left shouted, pointing outside the window opposite. "Across the street."

"Looks like a goddamned robbery," someone else called.

I heard the silence transform as the sounds of concerned chatter filled the restaurant. I saw people start to stand, some of them heading toward the fire escape. In the distance, I heard sirens, but that might not necessarily be anything to do with this incident. Sirens were just part and parcel of living in New York.

And then I saw it myself.

There were three people dressed all in black in the supermarket across the street. One of them was pointing a gun right at the terrified young cashier, who struggled to open up the cash register. There were other shoppers on the floor, all of them crying. A dad held his daughter in his arms, reassuring her that everything was going to be okay.

Then, I saw something even more horrifying.

As I looked around Pazza Notte, I realized that the remaining people in here were looking at me. They were looking at me not with hope but with fear. Fear at the realization that I wasn't who I used to be. In their eyes, I was just a normal person now, so there was nothing I could do to help the people across the street. I saw the looks of hope dying on the faces of so many, and I knew right then that the choice I'd made to keep my powers secret, the decision and promise Cassie and I had pledged together, was turning me into a bastion of fallen hope.

Sure, there were other ULTRAs out there, but nobody was *that* serious about maintaining world peace. That soon got boring after a day or two.

And sure, the world might be a much more peaceful place now in general than it used to be. But what about when it fell apart? What about when hope was truly stretched and challenged? What then?

I felt Ellicia's hand tighten around mine.

Then I saw Cassie staring at me.

She didn't have to say anything, as the background noise of shouting and wayward gunfire filled the supermarket across the street. I knew from the way she was looking at me that she wanted us to go over there. She wanted us to help. She wouldn't do it alone. She didn't believe in her own strength enough to act alone.

She wanted me by her side.

But I just felt sick.

I felt sick at the thought of going across the street and exposing myself as a Hero—as an ULTRA—once again.

I felt sick at the thought of the news stories and the Facebook posts and the tweets and the interviews and the media attention and the scrutiny and the—God, the whole damned lot of it.

I didn't want to be an ULTRA anymore.

I just wanted to be Kyle Peters.

Normal Kyle Peters.

I'd done a good job of it so far. I just had to keep on going.

"We need to—" Cassie started.

I shook my head.

I couldn't disguise the shame I felt when I shook my head. I know, I know. It made me despicable. Maybe it even made me villainous. It probably makes you not like me very much. Fourth wall breaker, sure, but let's be honest here—I'd made enough of a dick-move to warrant a fourth-wall break.

I saw the tears building up in Cassie's eyes as more flashes came from across the street. When I looked across, I noticed no one had been shot. The gunmen were just using the bullets to put the frighteners into their hostages. But the police were surely on their way now. And the way these guys were kitted out, they weren't going to give up without a fight.

They were going to use those guns as weapons.

And here I was, trying to resist the ice spreading down my fingers, all because I was too much of a baby to accept the powers I'd been given—to live with the hand of cards I'd been dealt with.

"I'm going," Cassie said.

I walked over to her and grabbed her arm. A few people looked at us, confused. "You can't."

"I have to," she said. "This—this is exactly the kind of situation we're supposed to be fighting. So we get over there. Both of us, Kyle. You know it's the right thing to do. You... you know we can't just let this happen."

I felt my jaw tense. I felt tears building in my eyes. I looked around the restaurant, looked at the pale, confused faces. I saw some hope returning to the eyes of some of them. The hope that perhaps Cassie was suggesting we *did* still have powers after all. That we were going to be able to end that situation across the road before it really took a hold and got nasty.

Instead, I held my breath and intensified my focus on Cassie.

I saw her shake her head. "Sorry."

Then she closed her eyes and went to spark her powers.

I waited for the purple electricity to climb up Cassie's arms. She waited, too.

But no electricity climbed up her arms.

None at all.

That's because I was holding my breath, grinding my teeth, and putting all my energy into repressing Cassie's powers and keeping them from surfacing.

I felt my eyes straining as Cassie pushed back harder against me. All while this was happening, I heard footsteps charging toward the supermarket. I heard the police shouting at the gunmen to stand down. I saw the flashing blue lights, and the more I tensed to hold back Cassie's powers, the more I tasted blood at the back of my throat.

"Don't do this," Cassie said. "Don't... don't do this."

I regretted what happened next.

Something so subtle that nobody even noticed I'd caused it. Nobody could possibly notice I'd caused it.

I clicked my fingers.

My sister passed out.

I caught her before she hit the ground. I wiped some of the blood from her nose.

And as I held her, I felt nothing but total shame.

I'd done this.

I'd caused this.

All because I didn't want the truth to come out.

All because I didn't want to be a hero anymore.

5

Hank White stuck his shovel into the dirt and hoped for better luck.

It was getting late, as it always seemed to be when he was digging recently. It'd been a scorcher of a day, the first real sign of Australian summer creeping up. He could just imagine going to Melbourne and smelling the fumes of barbies in the air. Mmm. Just the thought of a burger on a bun laced with cheese was enough to make him salivate, especially having not eaten for eight hours.

But he had to keep on digging.

He wasn't going to be having a barbie tonight.

He listened to the sound of the crickets. Other than that, it was perfect silence out here in the Outback. Not true Outback, of course. That was way too far a drive from the cities. But it was Outback enough compared to his usual home comforts.

Well. "Comforts" wasn't exactly the word for his tiny bedsit that he lived in with Anita.

He stuck his shovel deeper in the ground and pulled away some more soil. He felt sweat dripping down his forehead. His button down shirt barely clung on to him. He'd lost a lot of weight lately. He was losing weight when he'd quit his job as a bank teller with stress, and he'd kept on losing it as he failed to find another job, and as the bills piled up on his doorstep.

And then suddenly he didn't have a doorstep. He was in a condo, taking a severe downsize. Anita and he used to have a dog too, called Bruce, but they'd had to re-home Bruce because the landlord wouldn't allow pets. Hank didn't have anyone else to look after Bruce. He had no family. No friends. The ones he did have, he'd drifted from this last two years since his economic collapse. Anita had a job as a receptionist in a posh hotel, but that only just paid the rent and a little more. They were struggling. No doubt about that.

Anita nagged on at him to grow up and get a proper job again, but she didn't understand. Not really. Being a metal detectorist was his passion. He'd been into it when he was growing up, remembering the thrill of finding a dollar coin and spending it on sweets with his friends. But like all passions, life had got in the way. He'd grown up, and he'd grown numb to the world around him.

Since he'd quit his job, he'd rediscovered his passion.

He dug down further. He could taste the sweat on his lips. Hank wasn't exactly getting rich from his metal detector work. Most of what he found was just old bits and pieces. He liked making things too, so he handcrafted a few chairs and tables that Anita insisted were too ugly for the lounge, but hey, she was sitting on them so that was something. But every now and then, he found something of real value. Antiques. Car parts. Old phones that had been tossed aside with smashed screens, which he'd just gone ahead and fixed and resold. Not a killing, but enough to treat Anita to a nice meal every once in a while. Enough to keep her happy. Enough to—

(*Buy some more time before she leaves you forever*)—

No. He couldn't think like that. Anita loved him, and he loved her. They'd been childhood sweethearts. Gone to school together, gone to college together. They'd been there for one another even when times got tough.

They were here together now, and they were staying together for good.

And one day, Hank was gonna find something that'd make them rich again. He was gonna be on one of those programs on TV, and the news. And he was gonna inspire a whole new wave of metal detectorists.

He hoped today could be his lucky day.

But he'd been digging this same spot for hours now and still he hadn't reached whatever the hell his detector was beeping at.

He stopped, leaned back against the sand and looked up at the sky. He wondered what'd happen if someone came along and buried him right now. Or if he couldn't climb his way back out, so he'd be left here to fry in the sun. He wondered if anyone would really notice. There was Anita, sure. But would she really feel it anymore? Would she really care?

He wiped his forehead and let go of a sigh.

He didn't want to get another job because of the feeling he got in his chest whenever he thought about another inane day at the office. Sometimes it felt like he was having a heart attack. Other times, like someone was squeezing his lungs so tight he couldn't breathe.

Most of the time, though, Hank just felt total dread. Like something bad was coming. Something he couldn't describe. He just knew he had to get away from it. He had to run.

He looked down at where he'd been digging and in the last of the day's light, he saw something glinting.

He narrowed his eyes and reached down. He moved some of the sand away, brushing it back.

There was something here.

Something metal.

And he got the opposite feeling to the one when he went to work. A weird feeling. A feeling he wasn't used to, not anymore.

Hank White felt *excited.*

He kept on digging. Maybe it was some kind of old artifact. Some evidence of alien lifeforms. Damn, what if it was a UFO? A government experiment? A...

When he saw what it was, he couldn't help but collapse and laugh.

It was an old CD rack. An old goddamned CD rack buried here thirty feet down in the dirt of the outback. He felt tears then, as his laughter got more hysterical, the sand filling his eyes. He didn't care anymore. All of a sudden, he saw the ridiculousness of everything, and he didn't care about a thing.

A CD rack.

Maybe he'd get a dollar for it if he was lucky.

A dollar for hours of work.

A dollar for...

He saw something else, then.

It was only small. But when it caught his eye, Hank got the feeling that this was something different. Something... hell, something *important.*

He brushed away the sand, and he lifted the object out of the earth.

He looked down at it, a lump in his throat intensifying, his hands getting shaky.

It was round. Perfectly round, pretty weighty, and totally shiny, like it was brand new. It rested in the palm of Hank's hand, around the size of a tennis ball.

But it didn't look like anything Hank had ever seen.

He held it in his hand a few seconds. Then he put it into his coat and he started climbing his way out of his hole.

He felt like he'd found something of importance. He didn't know what it was, and maybe he'd never fully understand the true level of its importance, but he knew he had something special.

He didn't bother taking the CD rack along with him.

6

I sat beside Mom's grave and felt my eyes welling up, just as they always did.

It was a quiet afternoon. Still warm for September, but there were signs that fall was on the way now. Some of the trees were starting to show early shades of orange. There was an overall feeling of sleepiness to Staten Island, just before the rush in the build up to Thanksgiving.

Except I didn't want to think about Thanksgiving, especially if Mom wasn't going to be here to celebrate it.

I swallowed a lump in my throat and reached over to Mom's headstone. It still felt surreal, sitting here, looking at my mom's name staring back at me. That's all she was now. Mary Peters. Ten letters. That's what she'd been reduced to.

But to me, she was three letters. She was Mom.

And I missed her so, so much.

I listened to the breeze against the trees. I liked coming here when I was going through something tough. I didn't do anything weird like talk to the grave. I didn't say anything, or do anything for that matter.

All I needed was to sit here, to spend some time here, and to decompress in the company of Mom.

She'd been so tough. She'd been so positive. I idolized her.

And now she was gone.

I leaned closer to the headstone, not really caring about getting dirt on my jeans. I sat there and felt the sun against my skin. The rest of the cemetery was empty. I preferred it when it was this way. Sometimes, weird as it sounded, if I focused enough, I really believed I could hear Mom's voice talking to me, telling me everything was okay. That I was tough and I could handle whatever was going on in my life because she hadn't gone anywhere, not really.

I knew it wasn't true. I knew Mom was gone. Long gone.

And not in the way Cassie went away, either. Because Mom didn't have abilities. There was no mistaking what'd happened to her.

She'd died. She'd passed away.

She'd left way too early and hadn't even known her daughter had returned.

I wanted her here now. I wanted her to tell me what to do. Hell, even if she shouted at me for being such a wuss, told me to get myself together and start acting like a man, I just needed to hear *something* from her.

But all I heard was silence. All I heard was the breeze carrying the leaves across the cemetery.

All I heard was nothingness.

I stayed there a while. Stayed perched by the grave.

I wasn't sure how long I was there, but it felt nice to just pretend I didn't have any problems. To picture myself when I was younger, laughing as Mom pushed me on the swings, holding onto the handles for dear life. Even though I'd screamed as I'd climbed higher, terrified I might plunge off the edge of the swing and into the air, I still knew I was okay, deep down. I knew I was fine. Because Mom was there for me. She had my back. Always.

I'd felt Mom's death harder since stepping back from my powers, weirdly. I dunno what it was. Maybe I'd been distracted by the whirlwind of being an ULTRA that I just hadn't had time to process her death properly. I'd been too busy saving the world a number of times to let personal matters get in the way. I'd stepped up, just like I knew I should.

But there was only so long you could delay grief.

And when it hit you, it really hit you.

I was starting to understand why Dad went so downhill when he thought Cassie had died, now.

I closed my eyes, pictured Mom's smiling face, and bathed in the perfect silence.

Then I heard footsteps approaching.

I opened my eyes and swung around, my nerves still on edge.

When I saw it was Cassie, I let go of my breath.

I turned around and looked back at the grave. I waited for Cassie to approach. I hadn't spoken to her since I'd made her pass out at the restaurant. I knew the shouting that I was going to get from her would come eventually.

I just didn't want it to go down at Mom's grave.

"I'm sorry for—"

"I'll pretend you didn't do a thing. For both our sakes."

I half-smiled at her, a nasty taste filling my mouth at the memory of what I'd done, then I nodded and turned back to the grave. "I just... All this. This ULTRA stuff. We've done enough of it. We should be allowed to have lives, too."

"You know, you aren't the only one who struggles."

"Huh?"

"I struggle. But there's loads of people who struggle. People flying airplanes struggle with the thought that they might make a mistake and bring the whole thing down someday. Celebrities struggle with making the right moves in public in case the paparazzi misinterpret something and bring their reputation crashing. But that doesn't mean they don't just *deal* with those responsibilities. What you're doing isn't dealing with them. It's running away from them. And you can't run forever. I swear to God, our responsibilities are gonna catch up with us sometime soon. And when they do, the fallout's going to be bigger than either of us can imagine."

I sighed. "The rest of the ULTRAs in the world now seem to be doing a decent enough job."

"They're doing a decent job, but they're reckless. They're without order. They need a leader. They—"

"No," I said.

"What?"

"I said no."

"You're... snappier than usual. Something else wrong?"

No point trying to hide the truth from my mind reader of a sister. "Ellicia's going to San Fran."

"She is? Damn. That's amazing. Right?"

"It is. But not for the two of us."

"I don't see why her moving anywhere is a problem when you can fly to the—"

"I don't want to fly. Because flying brings questions. And before I know it, people will be asking why I'm in San Fran one day and New York the next and it... it'll all just become one big mess."

"So you're just going to leave her?"

When I heard the words and prepared to say my words, I hated myself a little more than I already did. "I'm thinking maybe it's for the best."

Cassie didn't lecture me. She didn't have a go at me, as I expected. She just sighed and shook her head. "See what giving up your responsibilities is doing to you? It's not magically giving you some new life. It's taking everything you care about away."

She put a hand on my shoulder.

"If you really aren't ready to embrace your powers, I guess I can't make you. Only I'm not gonna hide forever. But Jesus, Kyle. Get a job, or go to college or something. Just... just start growing up. Seriously."

Cassie started to walk away. Her words were biting. But they were exactly what I needed.

"You're right," I said.

She stopped and turned around. "About what?"

I saw the hope in her eyes and just had to go and extinguish them. "About going to college. I think I'm gonna look into taking some classes again. Picking up my education. Before my brain melts."

It wasn't the answer Cassie wanted to hear, but it was something. She smiled a little. "Good. I'm holding you to that."

She walked away.

I stood by the side of Mom's grave. I looked at it and I smiled. Even though she hadn't spoken, it felt like she'd spoken through Cassie. I was going to get my life in order. I was going to start again.

I looked up at the sky and I wondered if she was out there somewhere, watching down.

For a split second, I wondered about Orion, too. And I wondered about Daniel Peters. And I wondered about Saint.

But that momentary thought didn't last long.

I couldn't let it last long.

I had a new life to start now.

A normal life.

7

Hank White stood at the side of the road in the middle of nowhere and started to question whether he was completely insane after all.

It was the middle of the night. Five past twelve, to be precise, so technically morning. He was on a long empty stretch just outside of Narrandera. It'd taken him a while to get out here. There'd been a hold up back at the nearest town, which worried him because he didn't want to be late for his appointment.

Because from what the woman on the phone said, this could be an appointment that changed his fortunes—changed his life —for good.

Rain lashed down on Hank as he stood fifty feet from his car. That was weird, too. One of the requests the woman had made on the phone was that he was fifty feet from his vehicle. When he asked her why, she said it was just a weird kind of procedure of theirs. They were making a big deal; they didn't want to risk anything going awry.

So here Hank was, standing in the rain, five minutes late

and wondering whether he'd screwed up his damned opportunity to make a killing all along.

All around him in every direction, darkness. He figured he'd at least see headlights approaching from the distance when the woman and her people arrived to make the exchange. He could hear clicking noises, and weird shuffling by the sides of the road and thought of how many creepy crawlies and vicious animals might be just feet away from him. The thought made his skin tingle.

He just hoped he hadn't screwed this deal up by being late. He hoped he hadn't dug his family into another goddamned hole, all because of his clumsiness and lack of responsibility.

He wiped some of the pouring rain from his forehead and thought back to the events of a crazy day. He'd got home with his discovery—the little metal ball—and right away, Anita said someone had called. Someone very interested in making an offer for something he had. He'd called back and immediately he'd got an answer, without a single dialing tone. A woman. She sounded British, although there was a hint of Aussie to her accent. Maybe an ex-pat. She wouldn't be the first British ex-pat to make her way to Australia.

She told him she'd heard he had something very valuable. He'd played hard to get at first, haggling and everything. But then she'd said she was putting a serious seven-figure offer on the table. Life changing money. And at that point, all reason slipped out of Hank's mind. All questions and doubts about how this woman knew he had the metal ball, about how she'd found out about it, about what it even was... all of them slipped away, and Hank saw dollar signs.

He was going to be rich.

He was going to move Anita out of that goddamned awful bedsit.

They were going to start their lives again, for real, and Hank wouldn't ever have to think about working again. Ever.

But now here he was, five minutes late, and there was no one to be seen.

He waited. He figured he had nothing better to do. He thought about going back to his car and sitting in there for a while, but he was drenched as it was so it wasn't exactly gonna make a world of difference.

The longer he waited in total darkness, the more agitation crept into his system. The more the tightness wrapped around his chest, and squeezed on his lungs—

(*You're useless you're a waste of space always have been always will be just kill yourself already*)—

No!

He couldn't think about killing himself. That was a damned nasty thing to think about. No, he was gonna fight. He was gonna wait here, and he was gonna seal this deal. Worst case scenario? They didn't show up, and he went back home. He'd just call them again. Tell them he wanted more money. Or if this thing he had really was so valuable, then maybe he could sell it on to someone else. Yeah. That was a point. If one party were offering seven figures for it, then they wouldn't be the only group after it. There would be others.

That's it. Deep breaths, Hank. You're not gonna screw this up. For once in your goddamned life, you're not gonna screw something up.

As he waited longer, he found himself reaching into his pocket and feeling the metal ball. It was so smooth. Like the softest metal he'd ever felt. He didn't want to get it out in the rain because he didn't want to risk breaking it or damaging it. But something told Hank that this metal wasn't going to be damaged anytime soon. It might've looked new, but it was so buried under the earth in such a weird location that Hank couldn't possibly see how anyone had lost it anytime recently.

It had to be old.

And it had to be special.

He was starting to think about going back to the car again when he became aware of movement right behind him.

Not just any old movement.

Footsteps.

Human footsteps.

When he turned around, he saw a dark silhouette, barely visible in the light of the stars.

"Hank White?"

When he heard the voice, he immediately recognized it as the woman from the phone. The nameless woman. That was weird, too. Prospective business client, and she weren't even willing to give her name? There was something very off about all this. Something very secretive.

Hank stood tall and took in a deep breath to make himself look more assertive. "Speaking. And you are?"

"There's no need for formalities here. Do you have it?"

Hank's automatic reaction was to reach into his pocket and hand it over to this woman right away. She was offering serious money, and he couldn't wait to get his hands on it.

But something made him hesitate.

"Do you have what you promised me?"

The woman didn't respond.

"The money," Hank said. "Seven figures, you said."

"Name a figure."

"What?"

"Name a figure."

Hank wasn't sure he liked this much freedom. He was tempted to go for the max of $9,999,999. But the polite guy inside won over, of course. "Shall we say um... um, four million?"

"Make it forty," the woman said.

Hank's jaw almost dropped off. "What?"

"Forty million. That's more in the region of what this item is worth."

Hank couldn't believe what he was hearing. This woman could've said anything to him right now, and he'd follow her orders.

"So do you have it?" the woman asked. "You show me yours, I'll show you mine. Then we'll figure out the best way to exchange."

Hank felt skeptical, but that skepticism was drowned out by the thoughts of all the things he could do with forty million dollars. He could buy a mansion. Buy a posh car. He and Anita could get a dog again. Hell, they could get ten dogs, and they could buy Bruce back from his adoptive owners and reset. Start again.

So that vision, that fantasy of the future, forced him to pull out the metal ball. Hold it up.

It glinted in the starlight.

"So where's the—"

He felt a sharp pain in his back, and he immediately dropped to his knees.

He didn't understand what was happening. It was only at that point that he'd noticed someone else was behind him. And something was spreading up his back. Something warm. Something soothing. It was sneaking through every muscle in his body and making them calm. Making them... still.

The woman leaned toward Hank. "I'm a woman of my word. I will make sure your wife gets that forty million. Truly."

Then she reached for the metal ball.

And as much as Hank tried to grip hold of it, his visions of an ideal future slipping away along with his consciousness and strength, he just couldn't hold on anymore.

He had to let go.

He had to give in.

"You should be grateful," she said, her voice blurring into the background. "I just put a forty million life insurance clause over your head. Your wife can finally quit her job and follow her dreams. Doesn't that make you happy?"

Hank couldn't deny he felt happy.

For the first time in a long time, as his hearing faded, then his sense of smell, then his touch, he felt like he'd done something selfless for Anita. Like he'd taken on responsibility for his family.

And as his vision faded away, his last image was of Anita's smiling face when she found out they could move out of that shitty bedsit and to somewhere fresh.

They were starting again.

Hank's metal detector passion had finally, finally come through.

They were going to be millio...

His vision totally blackened, his thoughts went blank, and Hank slumped down onto the road.

"Make it look like suicide," Moira said.

She looked down at the metal sphere and couldn't help smiling.

Because what she held in her hands made her the most powerful woman in the world.

8

I wanted some downtime at the arcade with Damon and Avi, but I forgot that downtime in a public meeting place for geeks wasn't so easy when you were so recognizable.

It was the middle of the afternoon on a Monday, so, in theory, this place should be empty. But it was still the tail end of the summer vacation, so geeks like me were making the most of their last opportunity to game with a load of fellow geeks before the return to normality.

Only today was a special day.

I felt it when I walked through the door. It'd gone warm outside again, so I felt a little sweaty and sticky, which always put me in a bad mood. The arcade had just gone silent. People had stopped gaming. They'd turned around, looked at me, looked at their friends, and a sense of stasis had kicked in.

Then they'd all charged toward me shouting and cheering, begging me for selfies, sticking phones in my face, as well as comics. Yeah. I had my own comic now. I'd done a deal with one of the major companies to fictionalize my adventures. I think some people read those comics and believed everything that happened in them. Never underestimate the ability to confuse fiction and reality in the twenty-first century age of information.

Damon patted me on the back as the mob approached. "Good luck, man."

"Don't leave me with these people."

Avi laughed. "Bro, they're your fans."

"But I don't feel comfortable."

"Just enjoy it," Damon said, grinning. He clearly loved how uncomfortable this whole thing made me. He held out his arms as he walked off toward the new House of the Dead VR game. "Hey. If I'd kept hold of my powers, I'd be lapping it right up. Make the most of it, man. Now I've got some VR zombies to shoot."

I looked around at the smiling crowd, the smell of their stale sweat hanging in the air, and I just about managed a smile back.

But that wasn't the easiest thing to force.

I signed comic after comic, shook sweaty hand after sweaty hand. Some people asked me what it was like taking Saint out. Others asked me what I'd done with him, whether they ever had to worry about him returning. One guy, with an acne-ridden forehead and glasses so thick his eyes looked the size of tennis balls, led me to the back of the arcade and introduced me to a video game I didn't even know existed.

ULTRA: The Last Hero.

"You get to play as you," the guy said, chuckling after every word. "Right from when you're a kid. Then there's the fight with Nycto. But the best bit's when you get to choose between saving your mom or your dad. And whoever dies, you go apeshit. It's genius."

I felt a little sick and dizzy. I'd okayed this game? A game that fictionalized the most traumatic event of my life?

"That's—that's great," I said. "I need to... the bathroom."

"You okay, Glacies? You're looking pale."

"I'm not Gl... I'm fine. Really. I just need some air. That's all."

I battled my way through the army of people. I just wanted to get to the bathroom and get out of here. I didn't want to face the reality of this crowd. And, shit. This was a crowd of fans that thought I *didn't* have any abilities. If they knew I did... then how in the name of hell would I ever be able to go out and do the things I wanted to do? How would I ever hope to be normal?

I reached the door to the bathroom corridor, opened it up.

That's when I saw them.

It was only for a fraction of a second. Literally a case of them being there one second then gone the next.

But I saw the dark shadow at the opposite end of the corridor, and I got the feeling that someone was watching me.

The door to the corridor slammed shut as it swung behind me, making me jump out of my skin. I walked down the corridor slowly, fingers tingling, heart racing. I wanted to call out to see if anyone was down there. But more than that, I just wanted to get to the bathroom. Take a breather. And then get the hell out of here.

I walked into the bathroom. I took a cubicle, the feeling that I was being watched still overwhelming. When I looked up at the ceiling, I saw some graffiti beside a hole in the panels.

No peeping.

And beside it, someone else had written in red pen: *Why? ;)*

I looked back down and saw feet under the cubicle door.

Before I knew it, the door burst open, and someone threw a fist at me.

I acted on instinct. I grabbed the attacker's hand and froze it in an instant.

Then I teleported through him, behind him, kicked him in the back and onto the bathroom floor.

As I stared down at the mess, still in shock at what had happened, I didn't notice the other guy until the last second.

I spun around and grabbed his chest, but it wasn't quick enough. He fell onto me and tried to push a long metal rod at me.

I took a breath, composed myself, and I pushed that metal rod back, using my mind to force it away. I clenched my teeth together, increasing my focus. The metal rod bent and moved toward the guy's head.

He dodged it. Slipped out of its way.

Then I grabbed him with my mind and lifted him into the air.

I opened up a wormhole on the bathroom floor.

And I tossed him and his friend into it.

When they'd gone, I collapsed onto my knees. I tried to compose myself. Tried to steady my breathing. Someone was after me. Two people. And they weren't just random idiots, clearly. They had weapons, so they'd been sent by someone.

And if they'd been sent by someone, that meant someone knew I still had my abilities.

Someone knew I wasn't being completely honest.

I took a few deep breaths. They were gone now. They couldn't hurt me. I just had to get out of here and go back home. I couldn't ever come back, either. It was just too risky.

I walked over to the bathroom door and went to step outside.

If I wasn't as rusty as I was right now, I might've sensed there was someone out there waiting for me.

I might've been able to stop them pressing a metal rod to my chest, sending a burst of electricity surging through my body.

And I might've been able to stop myself falling to the floor, cracking my head on the hard, trodden down carpet, and slipping away into unconsciousness.

9

I opened my eyes, but I might as well have kept them closed.

It was pitch black. So pitch black that I wasn't sure I'd be able to put myself in as much darkness if I squeezed my eyes together. My head felt dizzy, and I could taste vomit. My throat was sore, and my body felt weak and woozy. Part of me wanted to fight against the darkness, fight against whatever the situation I was in *was*.

But most of all, my body just wanted to give up. To accept the darkness. To sink down into its warm arms and let it surround me, returning to sleep.

And then I remembered what happened.

I was at the arcade. I'd been there with Damon and Avi. I'd got caught up in a crowd of geeks, who were way too interested in me for me to be anywhere near comfortable. I'd seen a video game re-enactment of my life and it had freaked me out, so I'd done a runner to the bathroom.

Only the bathroom plan hadn't turned out such a great idea. I'd been attacked. I'd used my abilities to stave off that attack.

Then when I'd gone to leave the bathroom, someone had

stepped around the door and electrocuted me, rendering me powerless.

I tasted that vomit tang growing stronger in my mouth as the urgency of my situation grew. Why was I always going and getting myself caught like this? Whatever. I had to get away. It might be a struggle, but I wasn't keen on sticking around in... well, mystery dark place, wherever mystery dark place was.

I went to move.

That's when I realized I was tied down.

I tensed my fists, tried to freeze the ties around my arms and my ankles, tried to snap them with the full force of my abilities.

I couldn't.

A sickening realization hit me in a strong tidal wave of force. Someone had hunted me down. They'd put me in here. And the fact that my abilities didn't seem to be working right now meant that someone was repressing them in some way.

Which, in turn, meant that whoever had captured me knew I was lying about my abilities.

They knew I was still an ULTRA. They knew I still had powers.

They knew I was still Glacies.

They knew the truth.

I took a few deep breaths and closed my eyes. I couldn't freak out. I had to stay calm and composed. I'd been in situations like this in the past, and I'd found my way out. I couldn't act rash. I had to think. If my abilities were being suppressed, then how could I break free of ties around my arms and legs? Sure, the suppression of my abilities might be strong, but surely my abilities themselves were stronger?

It might take it out of me. It might not be easy. But I was going to have to find a way to break out of this situation one way or another.

I gritted my teeth together and focused on the power, right

at my core. Sometimes, in the quietest moments, I could feel my abilities, like they were an organ in my body. I could feel their silent electricity floating through me. I wondered, if I could feel it, maybe others could detect it too. Maybe that's why I was here. Perhaps that's what had happened all along. I had been caught out. I'd tried to outrun my past, but all I'd really been doing was jogging away from it limply and pathetically. Now here I was, the real me, lying back in the darkness, unable to—

"Turns out you're not so powerless after all, hmm?"

The gruff old voice made me freeze, and not in the ability way, unfortunately. It sounded like it came from in front of me. *Right* in front of me. And then I realized I could smell the sour breath of someone just inches from my face, and I knew for certain then I wasn't alone.

"What's wrong? You gone quiet on me all of a sudden?"

"Let me out of here."

I heard a chuckle. This guy, whoever he was, sounded old. "I'm afraid that's not going to happen, Kyle Peters. Not until we've had a proper conversation."

Right on cue, a mass of lights switched on. I closed my eyes, the light so blinding that it made my head hurt. When I opened them again, I tried to focus on the man standing over me as he came into view.

When he did, I realized my suspicions about him being old weren't far off the mark at all.

He looked ancient. Wrinkly. Thin white hair. He was hunched over, and he looked as if he could fall apart if someone so much as flicked him. He couldn't have been more than fifty kilos, which was even more dramatic considering how tall and lanky he was, even bent over. His fingers were long and bony, and his knees protruding against his scruffy gray trousers.

"I would offer a hand," the man said. "But I don't think shaking your hand is an option right now."

I looked down and realized I was tilted forward on a kind of table, my arms and legs tightly held back to this surface, whatever it was, wherever it was. I looked around at the rest of the room. It was pretty large, with white tiles all over the walls. It reminded me of one of those rooms people with issues are put in when they're considered a threat to society, only these walls weren't lined with anything soft.

"My manners. I apologize. I don't get to meet many new people anymore. I'm Michael Williamson. You probably haven't heard of me, which I always find terribly unfair."

"Yeah well life's shit. Not everyone gets to be a celebrity."

"I'm no celebrity," Michael said, a smile of yellow teeth (at least those that were still remaining) stretching across his face. "But you should know that if I weren't here, then you wouldn't be an ULTRA right now, and neither would anyone else."

I frowned. I wasn't sure whether to take this guy seriously. It was a bold claim, but it was a claim I had to consider. "You... Wait, you created the ULTRAs?"

Michael turned around and walked away, hands behind his back. "It was the seventies. The Second World War was long over, but there were new issues. The Cold War was intensifying. The Soviets were growing more powerful. The Vietnam War was in full flow. The world was staring Armageddon in the face. But there was a reason the Cold War never became a truly Hot War."

He turned around and smiled at me.

"And that reason was America's completion of the Hero program. A program that had been researched for years prior, actually. The first Hero tests predate the Second World War, even. But it came to fruition with my project. With Project Beta. Then, eventually, just over fifteen years ago with the Heroes that followed. Your biological father included. Orion."

My mind spun. He could've just been a batty old man, but

there were pride and sincerity to his words that made it hard to doubt him. "So... so what has that got to do with why I'm here now? Why you're keeping me captive?"

"I wanted your kind to be free. I mean, when I say your kind, you have to understand that I figured a way to get the Hero program into the bloodlines of those first individuals who had been gifted with their abilities. That wasn't the vision of the government. But it was something I wanted. An idyllic idea of the future, I imagine. The next stage in humanity's evolution. Only there was a catch. If I wanted to complete my project, I had to create a failsafe."

"A failsafe?"

"An off-switch. I was against creating it. But after the first conflict with Saint, I was convinced that the Failsafe had been lost. I made moves to make sure it disappeared and could never resurface. Even if it put all of humanity at risk, I wanted to let nature do its thing, as it should do. But now it pains me to say that it appears a second Failsafe has surfaced. It must've been a backup or an exact copy. But make no mistake about it. This Failsafe is in the hands of some dubious individuals."

I was so entranced that I'd pretty much forgotten I was tied down still. "This Failsafe. Why should I give a damn about it? And what does it have to do with anything?"

I saw a slight paleness stretch across Michael Williamson's face.

"Michael? What is it?"

"You should care about it," he said. "You should care about it very gravely. Because the Failsafe was designed in case of a major disaster. A major accident."

"I don't understand."

"The Failsafe has the ability to destroy every single ULTRA in existence. It's the ultimate weapon of mass destruction. And it's just fallen into the hands of some very dangerous people."

10

"Are you okay? You seem to have gone a little... pale."

I leaned back against the chair, which Michael Williamson had kindly allowed me to sit in now he was convinced I wasn't going to burst out of here in a ball of ice. I wasn't sure what time it was, or what the weather was like outside. I was completely disoriented, growing used to the white walls of the room I'd been trapped in earlier, and the gray metal walls of this other room in here, which appeared to be some kind of office. There was a strong smell of food in the air, though, and I noticed a microwave on the floor below where Michael and I sat. I figured Michael must pretty much live here, secluded, totally cut off. Wherever *here* was.

"So the people who have the Failsafe. They're dangerous?"

I looked into Michael's eyes and I saw a hint of a smile, like he was relieved that I was finally acknowledging his presence, and his concerns. "I don't mean to use hyperbole. But rest assured, I am gravely concerned about what might happen should these people put the Failsafe to use."

"How do they put the Failsafe to use?"

Michael paused and looked away. "There is a place. Like a lock to a door. If you take the Failsafe to that place, turn the key so to speak, all ULTRAkind falls in an instant."

I pictured that horrible image. Not just myself. I didn't think about myself at all, really. But more Cassie. My sister. And the rest of the Resistance, who'd all gone their separate ways after the battle with Adam, but were still out there somewhere.

I tried not to think about the guilt I felt over the Resistance's split. I'd turned my back on them, all for an easy life. After that, they'd just collapsed.

"Would you like something to eat?" Michael asked.

I shook my head, as dry as my throat was and as roaring as my stomach was. "This... Failsafe. Why didn't anyone just activate it when the stuff with Saint went down?"

Michael rubbed his fingers through his thin, stringy gray hair. "Quite straightforward, really. The people in power were too afraid of giving up their own power. Because, sure, they could take down the ULTRAs. But then what do they have left? The American government's greatest military expense in history, gone in the click of a finger. What do you think that would say to the rest of the world?"

"The rest of the world almost wasn't a thing."

"Not true," Michael said.

I frowned. "How can you say it's not true? I was there. I fought in that battle. I took down Saint."

"Exactly. You did your job. There was a threat. Admittedly an unconventional threat. A dangerous threat. But the true purpose of the Hero program shone through. Because you won. Didn't you?"

I had to admit Michael had a point. "People died. Lives were lost."

"People always die. At least now we have a way to minimize the impact."

"You can never minimize the impact of death to someone who's lost. Ever."

Michael tilted his head to one side. "I suppose not. But we're trying."

He stood up then, with surprising agility for a man clearly as old as him. "What happened in the past is irrelevant. It's now we have to think about. The Failsafe has resurfaced, whether we like it or not. And some very dangerous people have got their hands on it."

"So you keep saying. What's so dangerous about these people?"

"They are a militia. A glorified gang, really. But as long as they hold that Failsafe, they hold the key to power."

"What have they got against the ULTRAs?"

"They can bide their time. Grow their armies. They can gain support. And when they're ready to use that Failsafe, they can topple ULTRAkind and become the most powerful force on the planet."

"Not bad for a glorified gang."

"Read some history books. You'll soon see it's the glorified gangs who always reign supreme in the end. But not this time. We can't allow that."

"'We'?"

"There's a reason you're here, Kyle."

"I guessed that much."

"You might've convinced the rest of the world your powers were gone, but I'm not as stupid as that. I know for a fact that powers as strong as yours don't fade that easily."

"I've seen it happen to others. It wouldn't be too ridiculous."

"You've seen it happen to others, have you? Really?"

"Damon. My best..."

I saw the look in Michael's eyes and I wondered whether Damon was being totally straight with me all along.

"But that's beside the point. You're here because, like it or not, you're still the strongest ULTRA in existence. And that means you are going to do what you have to do. Serve your... let's call it your moral duty."

"Which is?"

"You are going to retrieve the Failsafe from the militia. You are going to take it away from them. And then you are going to return it to me, where I can look after it in safety."

"And why should I trust you?"

"Huh?"

"Why should I trust you won't just destroy me and my kind?"

Michael's eyes watered right then. He shook his head. "I created you. In many ways, I am your father. Why on earth would I destroy my beautiful children when I didn't even *want* a failsafe creating in the first place?"

I pondered Michael's words. He had a point. If he'd created me, if he'd created all of ULTRAkind, then surely he was more trustworthy than some random criminals.

"I'm not sure I can do this," I said.

"And why on earth wouldn't you do this?"

"The world. They... they think I'm normal now. And I just... I guess I like that. I want to be normal. Being normal for a while's done me good."

Michael smiled. He wiped his eyes, and then held out a hand, resting it on my shoulder. "Kyle, you *are* normal. You are just growing up. That is a part of life everyone has to accept."

I swallowed a lump in my throat and felt my world falling apart once again.

"So what do you say?" Michael asked.

I took a few deep breaths. Ran through scenarios in my head. Should I? Shouldn't I? Did I have a choice, really?

In the end, I closed my eyes, took a final cleansing breath, and went with my heart.

"Where do I find the Failsafe?"

11

I hovered over the Australian Outback and had to admit, being Glacies again didn't feel all that bad.

It was night. The air was cold, way colder than the stereotypes about Australian weather suggest. But I supposed this was technically the desert. Scorching during the day, cool at night.

Probably didn't help that I had ice coming from my palms.

Or that I was dressed in nothing more than my Glacies gear.

I looked down at the compound in the distance. It was dark, but I could see in the dark now. I'm special, remember? One of the advantages of being super-special was the discovery that you had abilities beyond your understanding, sometimes. You just kinda had to let them happen. A list of them would've been nice, I had to admit.

The place was bigger than I expected, like some kind of warehouse. There were lots of black vans parked up around the front, and high barbed wire fences to keep anyone who might cross by this place out. It was totally dark, though. No lights or anything like that. I'd only recently learned I could see in the dark if I put my attention to it. Like, very recently. As in now.

The beauty of being an ULTRA. You're learning new things about yourself all the time.

Just a pity I wasn't keen on being an ULTRA anymore.

I could hear chatter down below, cutting through the otherwise silent Outback landscape. Well, I say silent. There were loads of crickets chirping away. More than I ever thought was possible.

I felt the tension in my gut as I hovered, invisible, down toward the compound. I took in deep breaths of the dry air, still hungry having not eaten for... well, Michael Williamson never actually told me how long he'd had me captive. He'd never told me who the people who captured me were, either. There were a lot of things he hadn't told me. Why me? Why did I have to be the one to retrieve the Failsafe? Did "because you're the strongest ULTRA" really cut it?

Whatever. I was here. And I was going to get the job done with as quickly as I possibly could, with as little fuss as I possibly could.

In. Get the Failsafe. Out.

Simple.

Right?

I lowered closer toward the compound. The nearer I got, the more aware I became that there were people right below me. Guards—dressed all in black. I became conscious that they might be able to see me. I hadn't used my abilities for so long that it felt like I was discovering them all over again.

I took some deep breaths, drifted further downward...

Then I saw a blanket of electricity sparkle right above the compound.

I lunged up back into the sky. I could feel my skin singeing, my invisibility faltering. Shit. There was some kind of trigger over this place. I'd hovered right into it.

"Did you see that?" an Australian accent called.

"Jeez, Martin. Not seeing things again are ya?"

"I swear. Something triggered the electricity. It could be him. He could be here already."

"Who?"

"You know who. You know damn well who."

I saw two men walk over to just under my position, where I hovered in the sky, trying to get my invisibility to cover me again.

They looked up. And for a moment, I swore one of them—must've been Martin—looked right into my eyes.

Then the guy with him nudged him and laughed. "See? Nothing there."

Then he lifted his rifle and fired up toward me.

I dodged the bullets and watched as a wall of electricity sparked just inches from me. I bounced around every shot, taking my time, steadying my focus, but I was rustier than I used to be. I wasn't as quick. I wasn't as—

A searing pain shot through my left leg.

It took all my composure, all my guts, not to scream.

"See?" the guy said, patting Martin on the shoulder. "Nothing."

The pair of them walked away as the blanket of electricity continued to crackle.

I gritted my teeth. The pain of being shot was worse than I remembered. I quickly hovered back to the side then put all my attention on healing my leg. It was painful. This wasn't what I signed up for. I should be at home, enjoying one of my final days with Ellicia before she went to college. Instead, I was fighting someone else's battle, all over again.

I healed my leg and floated back above the compound. I had no choice. I had to get in here. If I didn't, I was putting every ULTRA in existence at risk.

So I closed my eyes.

I didn't just make myself invisible. I made myself *non-existent.*

And then I appeared at the other side of the electric barrier.

I was surprised I'd actually got through it at first, still amazed by my powers. I'd got so rusty that I'd forgotten just how handy they could become.

But getting into this compound was the easy part, surely. The hard part was getting the Failsafe and then getting out of here.

The sooner I could get back to normality, the better.

I hovered just above the ground. I headed toward the doors of the compound, which two people stood guard by. I was constantly aware that they might just look at me and shoot at any moment, and God knows how I'd react to another bullet.

But they didn't.

I was right beside them, and they didn't even glance at me.

I closed my eyes again and pictured the world behind the compound door. I could sense that there was someone right on the other side. A few people walking the corridors. All of them armed.

I thought back to those electric barriers.

What if they weren't just keeping something out?

What if they were keeping something *in?*

I didn't have time to dwell. I floated inside and headed down the corridor, keeping as low a profile as possible. The corridor was long, metal, and dark. I could smell grime. This place was in need of a serious clean.

But I wouldn't be sticking around here long anyway.

The further I got down the corridor, the more I started to doubt that I was in the right place. The Failsafe, if it were so powerful, wouldn't just be in here, would it? This group wasn't possibly as organized as Michael claimed they were, right?

And then I saw it.

It only just caught my eye, through a door on the right. But it was exactly as Michael described.

Small. About the size of a tennis ball.

Metal.

There could be no mistaking it.

It was the Failsafe.

I drifted toward it, creeped out that no one was guarding it. I looked down at it and I smirked. This little thing was really so powerful? This was the very thing that could end the lives of my entire species in an instant?

As I lifted it, feeling the smooth metal, I *felt* it. The weight of it. Not heavy in the conventional sense. But just a feeling like it was filled with something very special. Like it carried secrets I didn't, and couldn't, understand.

And then I heard footsteps behind me.

I turned around and saw eight people standing at the door.

All of them had guns.

At the front of the group, a woman with short blonde hair.

"Drop it," she said. "Immediately."

12

I held onto the Failsafe, fully aware that I was in deep, deep crap.

There were eight people opposite me, all but one of them dressed in black with their faces covered, all pointing rifles in my direction. Right in the middle of these people, a woman, with silvery hair. She was holding a pistol. Her face wasn't covered.

"You don't want to resist, Kyle Peters. I mean, I'd hate for the news about the truth to leak. The truth about your abilities. Wouldn't you?"

I knew right away what the woman was referring to and it knocked me sick. "You're threatening me?"

"Well, I think the public deserve to know that the world's most powerful ULTRA is still flying around the world with his powers intact, don't you?"

I shook my head, feeling a little bead of sweat slip down my forehead. "This Failsafe. It doesn't belong to you."

"And it doesn't belong to *you*, either. In fact, it especially shouldn't belong to you. Not with the kind of power you have."

"Because you really have good intentions with this Failsafe, do you?"

"Oh, I can assure you our intentions are very honest. It's about time the power balance was shifted back in favor of humanity. Your kind is dangerous, and you do not know what you're messing with. You had a good run. But now it's time to hang up your boots and accept your new masters. Or, don't. And face the consequences. But we will come after you. We will come after you and everyone you care about. Hard."

I'd been threatened lots of times. I'd had the people I cared about threatened lots of times. That was just part of my life now.

It still got to me. It still scared me, the thought of someone taking everything that mattered to me away.

But I'd heard enough threats to know when they were empty.

"The press will find out about you the moment you leave this place. The world will question why Kyle Peters hasn't been looking out for them all along. You'll never live a normal life because everyone will know you're nothing more than a liar and a coward. Or, you can hand over the Failsafe, and we'll go easy on you. A lot easier."

I looked down at the Failsafe. What was it worth? Was it worth me giving up who I really was? Would these people really use it, if they had to? Was I honestly the last hope in retrieving it?

Then I looked back up at the group. "I appreciate the offer. Really. But I think I've got a better idea."

I fired a sheet of ice at the group and teleported behind them, the Failsafe still in my possession. As I ran down the corridor, away from the compound, I felt bullets spraying around me, and I knew I was going to have to fight as much as I wanted to run.

I shot a few blasts of ice back at the crowd firing at me. I froze some of their bullets too and threw them back at them, taking them down with the flick of a finger. I hadn't seen the woman since I'd made a break for it. I could picture her now, calling the news, telling the media that I was still powered, and I'd been cowering from my responsibilities—my reality—for a long time.

I imagined the disappointed looks on so many faces. The faces of Ellicia. Damon. Avi. Dad.

I imagined the disappointed looks on the faces of all the people who'd idolized me, all the people who truly believed I still wanted to help them, but was limited by my new found condition.

I saw my entire life falling apart. Both as Glacies and as Kyle Peters.

And then I stopped when I felt someone smack me in the face.

I fell back. Hit the floor.

A man stood over me.

He lifted a rifle to my head.

I saw him pull the trigger. I saw the bullet moving out of the gun as if it was in slow motion.

But my focus wasn't completely on the gun.

My focus was on the Failsafe, which had slipped between my fingers.

I watched it tumble back down the corridor, back toward the woman and the people with her that were still standing.

It was going to be in her hands again.

Or I was going to have a bullet in my head.

I had a choice.

Well. I would've had a choice. If I wasn't an ULTRA.

I kicked the gun up in the air.

It spun around so quickly that it knocked the gunman in the chin, the bullet firing inches above my scalp.

The gunman spun around in the air and fell back onto the floor with a crack.

Then I turned around.

I could run. I could make it to the Failsafe.

But the woman and the people around her, more of them now, were getting ready to fire. I could take my chances, but it wouldn't be easy.

"Leave," the woman said. "Leave. Now. For your own good. You don't understand what you're getting involved in. Not fully."

I wanted to. I wanted to give up. I didn't want to fight.

But I shook my head. "Not happening."

Then, where the Failsafe bounced, I created a thick sheet of ice.

It acted as a shield from the bullets. Not forever, but just for now.

The main thing was, the Failsafe bounced off it.

I sprinted toward it.

Picked it up.

Ran back toward the door of the compound.

I heard the ice shield smash just as I threw myself through it and stepped outside.

I put my hands on my knees. I didn't have much time to stick around or catch my breath. I had to get out of here.

I lifted my head and went to run.

I didn't make it very far.

A bigger armed group surrounded me. At least fifty people.

All of them pointing their weapons at me.

All of them ready to fire.

13

I looked at the crowd of people pointing their guns at me and wished I'd never got involved in this damned mess in the first place.

I held on tightly to the Failsafe. The people opposite me were all shining flashlights at me, which were perched on the top of their rifles. I felt like I was a performer on a stage, only I wasn't up on stage by choice. I was here because I was a puppet. Not just for these people, but for Michael Williamson too.

I wanted to just get back to normality, but I'd jeopardized my hopes of returning to normality now. There was no doubt about that.

I just had to find a way to get away from these people as quickly as I possibly could.

"Final chance," a voice behind me said. When I turned around, I realized it was the woman who'd been leading the group earlier. She looked at me through steely eyes, her silver hair stark in the brightness of the flashlights. "I'm being incredibly lenient right now; I'm sure you'll agree. You can hand over the Failsafe, and we can forget this ever happened. Or you can resist, and I promise we will rain hell on you."

I heard something then. Helicopters, it sounded like. When I looked up, I saw them approaching.

"That'd be the media," the woman said. "I called them just in case. Gave some friends an anonymous tip about something big going down here. Wouldn't it just be great for them to see you as you really are?"

"You're just full of shit," I said.

The woman frowned as if she was staggered that an eighteen-year-old guy had just sworn. "What did you just say?"

"I said you're full of shit. All these threats. All these 'one more chances'. Sounds to me like you're the desperate one."

For the first time since meeting her, I saw the woman's face soften. A smile stretched across her cheeks. "You really want to test how full of excrement I am? You really want to believe that I'm being anything other than reasonable right now? Is that a game you want to play?"

I looked around at the crowd holding their rifles.

"Some of them have bullets, sure. Others have anti-energy pulses. Enough to take you down. And when they do, we'll take you in as our prisoner and we'll finish you."

"I'm not worried about that in the slightest."

"You should be," the woman said, the sound of the helicopter getting nearer. "I mean, I think you'll maybe dodge one or two anti-energy surges, sure. But thirty? Forty? Is that a chance you really want to take? A risk you seriously want to make?"

I swallowed a lump in my throat and I looked around at all the flashlights.

"I think so," I said.

I tossed the Failsafe up into the air.

I saw everyone's eyes rise up into the sky, watching it as it floated above.

And then I clapped my hands and I smashed every single flashlight pointing at me.

I bounced around each and every one of the gunmen as quickly as I could. I patted them all on the back in the space of seconds, sending all of them through wormholes, taking some of their guns away and throwing them off into the distance.

I kept on going and going, the Failsafe still dangling in the air, the woman's eyes still transfixed on it.

And then I shot over to it and grabbed it from the air.

Something happened, then. Something I wasn't expecting.

I felt something smack into my side and knock me back to the ground. Hard.

It took me a few seconds to recover my composure. To tune into my surroundings.

When I looked, I saw the Failsafe a few meters away from my position.

I crawled to it, eager to get my hands on it before the group from the compound could—

A heavy smack made the ground shake.

I felt dust in my eyes and became aware that a helicopter was flying just above.

And someone had just jumped out of it.

Someone dressed all in black. Ridiculously well built. His face covered with a black hood.

He was standing opposite me.

He didn't look like the media.

I had no doubt that this guy was an ULTRA.

And he was looking at the Failsafe with fascination.

With serious fascination.

14

I looked at the ULTRA standing opposite me and I had no doubt that this guy was one mean bastard.

The darkness was faintly illuminated by the light from inside the helicopter. My night vision was working faintly, too. As I lay belly-flat on the ground, the Failsafe between me and this... whoever it was, I felt for the first time like I was really up against it. I'd had a confidence about taking the Failsafe from the militia. A confidence that I was stronger than them, right from the moment I'd got here.

But this guy. Tall. Bulky. Covered in black armor and a black hood. Yeah, he was made of steel; hopefully, not literally. And if I'd learned anything in my time as an ULTRA, it was that a fight against one single ULTRA was way more draining than a battle with a thousand men.

The ULTRA stayed still for a few seconds. I heard the helicopter rotors slowing down. Beside me, I saw shuffling that caught my eye. When I looked, I realized it was the woman who'd led the militia. She was lying face flat on the ground, clearly struggling. Her head was bleeding. Something had happened when this ULTRA arrived. Some kind of shockwave when he'd jumped down from the helicopter and landed on the earth.

And now he was walking to the Failsafe.

I brushed myself down and stood up. "That's not yours."

The ULTRA stopped. There was a silence to him. A silent confidence, like he was saying so much in his looks and actions without actually saying anything at all. For a moment, I wondered if he could talk. I saw there were people behind him. People, not ULTRAs, by the looks of things, sitting in that helicopter with him.

I wondered if they spoke for him.

But then he opened his mouth.

"It is mine."

Then he carried on walking toward the Failsafe.

His voice was strong and booming. It made me feel even more intimidated, as much as I knew I really shouldn't judge a dog by its bark, so to speak. I cleared my throat in an attempt to sound more masculine too. "It belongs to someone else. It definitely doesn't belong to an ULTRA."

"Then why are you so keen to get your hands on it?"

I couldn't answer that question. I realized what this looked like. How was I so different to any other ULTRA? What made me so special and privileged that I thought I could go telling other ULTRAs that they couldn't have something because they were ULTRAs, when I was an ULTRA myself and clearly wanted it desperately?

"Just back off," the voice said. "Nobody needs to get hurt here."

I thought about backing off. I seriously did. I know, I know. Wuss. Wimp. Etcetera. But there was another logical reason why I was thinking about backing off. If this ULTRA got their hands on this Failsafe, then they surely weren't just going to use it to destroy ULTRAkind, because that'd mean destroying them-selves in the process, right?

I took a deep breath, a bitter taste on my lips, as I watched the ULTRA step closer to the Failsafe.

"You can take it," I said.

The ULTRA stopped. He looked puzzled by my words. Like he was expecting a fight.

"You can take it. But you can't use it. You *won't* use it. And if you even come close to using it, I'll—"

"You won't take it!"

The voice seemed to come out of nowhere. A woman's voice, high-pitched.

I recognized it as the woman who had led the militia.

Only I didn't have much time to think about that.

A blast of anti-energy surged from a rifle she'd grabbed from one of her fallen comrades and flew at the ULTRA.

I saw an opportunity opening up. An opportunity to lunge for the Failsafe while the ULTRA was otherwise occupied. I focused on it, tensed my eyes together, reached out for it with that invisible telekinetic arm I had.

It rolled toward me.

Rolled closer toward me.

And...

I was distracted by what I saw next.

The anti-energy blast hit the ULTRA.

But nothing happened.

It bounced off him. Bounced off him like it was nothing more than water.

He was tough. There was no doubt about that.

Hopefully just not too tough.

"You made a mistake, Moira," the ULTRA said, addressing the woman like he knew her. "A very grave mistake."

She looked at me. "Please. Don't let Catalyst take it. You don't know what you're—"

"And now you're going to pay for that mistake."

I saw the anti-energy rise from nothingness to the ULTRA called Catalyst's side.

I saw them sharpen like knives, hovering in the air.

All pointing at Moira.

And then I saw Catalyst fire them at Moira as she lay there on the ground.

I looked away. I couldn't watch what happened next.

But needless to say, seconds later, the militia leader called Moira wasn't with us anymore.

And a part of me couldn't help wondering if perhaps she was the lesser of two evils after all.

I refocused my attention on grabbing the Failsafe. But when I pulled it now, I saw Catalyst lifting a few more of those anti-energy shards with his mind and grabbing onto the Failsafe too, clearly boasting a strong form of telekinesis.

"Whoever you are, you've got nerve. But you're involving yourself in something way, way bigger than you and I. Something that you should allow. Because trust me, brother. You will reap the rewards."

I was surprised then that Catalyst didn't know who I was. He didn't recognize me. I longed to look into his eyes, wherever they were, hiding underneath that black hood.

But if he didn't know who I was, that meant I had something to my advantage.

"See, that's where you're wrong," I said.

I opened up a wormhole right between Catalyst and the Failsafe, which was rolling toward him.

"It's you that this is too big for. See you later, tough guy."

I wrapped the wormhole around the Failsafe.

Then I lunged upwards into a wormhole of my own.

I saw the anti-energy charges fly at me. I saw them inches from me. I felt their burning force singeing at my ankles.

And then I disappeared, away from the Outback, away from the compound, away from Catalyst.

When I re-appeared in Indonesia, the Failsafe was with me.

I knew what I had to do.

15

Catalyst knew the ULTRA who had stood against him was gone.

He couldn't see him. Not properly. Not with vision, anyway. He was blind. A horrible condition to be cursed with. The world was a beautiful place, supposedly. So everyone told him.

But it didn't seem like the world was such a beautiful place. Not with all the chaos. Not with all the conflict. Not with all the hunger and all the famine.

Catalyst longed for a better world. A world with order. A world where the real beauty that people told him existed behind all the ugliness returned.

The Failsafe was a big part of that plan.

He walked slowly away from the helicopter and to the spot where the ULTRA had disappeared. He knew the exact spot. He could smell the perspiration in the air. He could feel the slight warmth to the ground where someone previously stood. They say going blind heightens your senses. Well, imagine knowing nothing but blindness. You are missing a sense. Therefore you are born with heightened senses.

And they only heighten the longer you survive.

Catalyst crouched down and felt the dirt between his fingers. He felt anger building up inside. He'd misjudged his enemy. He'd expected him to back down. Should he have told him more about his plans for a beautiful future? Should his method of getting the Failsafe have been different? He wasn't sure. But he knew one thing for certain, now. He wasn't going to go easy on whoever had taken the Failsafe away from him.

"He just disappeared, man," a voice behind Catalyst said. Catalyst recognized it as the voice of the helicopter co-pilot. As soon as he'd got wind of the Failsafe's location, he'd paid off a couple of people to fly him into this compound, masquerading as the media. Poor Moira had slipped up there, bless her. It was a shame what he'd had to do to her. But she'd stood against him, and people who stood against him had to pay the price.

"We tried to stop him. Tried to help you. But—"

"Silence," Catalyst said.

And then it did go silent.

Both of them went silent. Completely silent.

He waited for the heavy thud of their bodies against the ground. He had, of course, caused a major bleed on the brain of each of them. It wouldn't be painful. They wouldn't feel a thing. It'd just be like they were falling into a long, sudden sleep.

Life was over for them, but they'd served him well in the final moments of their lives.

Well. Apart from allowing the Failsafe to slip out of his reach. Apart from failing to truly support and fight with Catalyst.

And for that, they'd had to die.

Although Catalyst was pretty certain they'd have died regardless of how this played out.

Catalyst lifted the earth to his lips. He tasted it. There was lycra there. Some kind of costume that his foe had been wearing. He would remember this taste, and he would remember the voice of the ULTRA who'd stood against him. He sounded young. Late teens. His voice didn't reverberate loud enough to suggest he was bulky. In fact, from all the signs the other senses had created, Catalyst could see a pretty clear picture of the man who'd stood against him and taken the Failsafe away from him.

Lanky. Tall. Slim.

He'd bear that in mind.

He remembered how he used to be a similar build when he was just a young kid, before he'd been kidnapped, tested on. He remembered the rapid muscle growth that followed. And the bigger his muscles grew, the more he became aware that his mind was strengthening, too.

He was nineteen when he killed his first man with his mind and realized he was special. Not just physically super-strong. But mentally tough, too.

He was telekinetic. He could make the ground ripple with a punch.

He was strong.

And the last eight years had been an exercise in getting stronger and stronger, waiting for an opportunity to rise where he could truly stand against those who had made his life hell.

Where he could finally be the powerful man he'd always craved.

And where he could get his revenge on those who had made his life a misery.

He heard a cough.

The cough snapped him out of his trance. His head immediately shot in the direction of the cough.

It was Moira. No doubt about it.

Moira was still alive.

Catalyst stood. He walked toward Moira slowly, making his bone-fracturing footsteps heavier and heavier.

He crouched beside her. He couldn't see her, but he knew she wasn't in a good way. He could smell the blood in the air, taste the charred flesh. He could hear her heartbeat pounding and pounding. He knew she didn't have long left.

"All this time searching for the Failsafe, our little rivalry blooming, and this is what it comes to."

"He's—he's—"

"Hush now, Moira. I enjoyed our rivalry, in truth. But now it's time for you to sleep."

"You'll never win. You'll never..."

Catalyst held his breath and tensed every muscle in his body.

Moira coughed a little more.

Then she went quiet.

Catalyst crouched there in the silence. He took deep breaths of the cool desert air. Soon, the sun would rise. The morning would arrive with searing heat. And when it did, this place would be nothing but a lost compound in the middle of the Outback. A ghost town.

Catalyst stood up. He looked into the sky.

He would find whoever had the Failsafe.

He would take back what was rightfully his.

And when he did, he would destroy the ULTRA who'd stood against him.

And every single person who was important to him.

He closed his eyes again, crouched down, and jumped into the sky.

One rival might have died down there on the dirt.

But now he had a new rival.

And he wasn't letting that rival slip out of his grasp.

16

I shot through the sky above the Pacific Ocean, the Failsafe tightly gripped between my fingers.

It was getting darker the further I traveled, as I moved away from the rising sun in one part of the world and into the deeper night of the rest of the world. At least I wasn't as cool, now. Honestly, if you're wondering why I'm flying and not just teleporting, you're making a valid point. The problem was with Michael Williamson. He'd told me that he didn't want to tell me where his hideout was, because giving up that kind of information was potentially dangerous for everybody. When I asked him why it was dangerous, he gave me some vague answer about needing to keep his very existence a secret. I asked him how he could so easily trust me, and he told me he just knew from the look in an ULTRA's eye when he had to worry about them. He hadn't seen anything in me to worry about yet.

But as soon as he did, he wouldn't hesitate to cut me loose.

A nice thing to tell someone you're trying to encourage to save the ULTRA species for you.

Anyway, Michael said he'd find me as soon as I had the Failsafe. Again, I wasn't sure how. But I just had to trust him.

A niggling voice in the back of my mind told me things weren't going to be all that straightforward.

But I ignored it and kept on moving, hoping Michael would find me sooner rather than later. I wasn't all that keen on playing the role of sitting duck. Not one bit.

I looked down as I flew through the sky. The Failsafe was so small. It was impossible to believe that something so small could be capable of so much destruction. But I'd seen the conflict it was causing already. I'd seen the showdowns between enemies, all after the same thing, and I knew I was just another fighter in that war.

I didn't understand the true ramifications of what I was doing. I didn't even totally understand why Michael Williamson was so sure that he alone could protect something so important.

All I knew was that he seemed like the lesser of several evils.

Definitely less evil than Moira.

And certainly less evil than that big ULTRA, Catalyst.

I remembered the way he'd addressed me. He didn't know who I was. And I had to admit, that gave me a weird kind of hope. Perhaps there were others out there that didn't know who I was. And now the militia had been dealt with, I was growing more confident about my ability to just sink back into the shadows once all this Failsafe business was dealt with.

I had another thought, too. Another dark thought.

What if I activated the Failsafe?

Or what if I kept it for myself? Used it to establish *my* power over everyone else?

It'd certainly bring order. It'd firmly establish me as a leader again. Hey, maybe it'd even stop people and UTLRAs from bothering me.

A dark thought, sure. Because activating it meant killing

myself and the rest of the ULTRAs on this planet, including my sister.

But that'd also mean no more worries.

No more responsibilities...

No. I was being stupid. Sinister, even. I wasn't willing to put the people I loved at risk. Especially when Damon might still have a trace of ULTRA in him. In fact, what was it that Michael Williamson alluded to with Damon? That ULTRAs never really lost their abilities? Could that mean Damon still had powers?

Nah. Not possible. If he did, there's no way he'd be keeping them under wraps. I'd known Damon many years, and that much was true.

I just had to trust my instincts. Get the Failsafe back to Michael Williamson. Restore order. If I had to fight and take down Catalyst, then so be it. He was tough, but I could handle him. And when I did, I'd go back to my normal, hero-free life, and leave Michael and the rest of the world to deal with the fallout.

No more ULTRA.

No more Glacies.

Just a normal life of college and studies and girlfriends and drinking and—

I was so lost in my thoughts that I only just realized I was being followed.

When I turned, I saw someone flying behind me. I didn't recognize them. Definitely not Catalyst.

I lifted my hands to fire at them and then I felt myself bump into someone.

As I struggled to hold onto the Failsafe, steadying myself in the sky, I became aware that there wasn't just one ULTRA chasing me.

There wasn't just another that I'd bumped into.

I was surrounded by ULTRAs.

"Kyle Peters," a short, chubby guy with a lisp said. "Or do you prefer Glacies?"

I tried to shoot myself away, but I felt something pulling me back.

Then I realized what it was.

I was trapped in some kind of invisible leash.

A leash that the bald guy was holding onto.

He smiled, his bare pot belly dripping sweat. His teeth were yellow, some of them missing.

"The name's Morgan, but my friends call me Fat Morgan. Fancy seeing you up here, using your powers. Now come along, son. You're about to make me very rich, my boy."

17

I looked at the pot-bellied pig of an ULTRA hovering opposite me and I was more than confident I could fight him off, as well as his band of cronies.

But something in me was holding me back.

Something was restraining me from doing what I really wanted to do.

"There's no point resisting," Fat Morgan said, grinning. "We know who you are. We know what you're capable of. And we know how little you'd like that getting out."

"You aren't shit to me."

Fat Morgan chuckled. "Oh, really? That confident, are we? Guys, he's really that naive and confident. Ain't that funny?"

I heard a few chuckles from the surrounding ULTRAs. Some of them I thought I recognized. One of them, a guy not much older than me, had tree roots wrapped all around him, sharp wooden branches sprouting from his hands. Another's hands were steaming, and I didn't want to risk being touched by them anytime soon.

I might not have known *exactly* who they were, but I didn't need to. Not really.

This was an ambush. This was some kind of setup.

And it was bad news for me.

That was literally the only thing I needed to know.

I tensed my fists and became aware of the Failsafe's heaviness so close to me. I couldn't lose it. If I lost it, then it'd be out there for someone else to find. But if I stayed here forever, I was certain that Catalyst would catch up with me eventually.

"I suggest you leave it out," I said. "Unless you want to get—"

"We know what you've got, Glacies."

I looked around at them then, one by one. They knew what I'd got? Did that mean...

"The Failsafe," Fat Morgan said. He nodded toward my pocket. "We know you've got it and we know what it's capable of."

"You don't know a thing."

"Yes, we do. And there's no point dancing around the real reason we're here. We want it from you."

"Well unfortunately for you, that isn't going to happen."

"Think about what kind of power that Failsafe holds. Just think about how powerful the owner of that Failsafe could be. And if that power isn't enough, well. They'll be goddamn rich for sure."

"See, that's not exactly the kind of talk that's encouraging me to just hand the Failsafe over."

I saw a smile stretch across Fat Morgan's chubby face. The wind, high up as we were, blasted against us, the air cool and thin.

"Then we're done talking," Fat Morgan said.

He clapped his hands together and sent a huge shockwave surging toward me. I put on the brakes, prepared to teleport myself away from here—

The shockwave hit me with force. A real literal kick of

energy to the teeth. I tasted blood right away, and felt my neck hurtle back as I floated there in the sky. I tried to recharge my abilities, to bounce back, all the while making sure the Failsafe didn't slip from my grip.

But the ULTRAs around me were just too fast. They kept on swooping down, charging into me, beating me and bruising me.

And I didn't even feel like I could fight back properly.

I felt dizzy and sick as I floated there in the sky, hit following hit following hit. I saw the truth right then, straight up. I wasn't as strong as I used to be. I wasn't the ULTRA—the Hero—I once was. Whether it's because I'd spent so long resisting my true identity that I'd lost the ability to fight like I did, or whether I was just weakening over time through lack of focus, I wasn't sure.

It didn't really matter. I was getting my ass handed to me.

I saw an opportunity right then, in the haziness of thought. There was a gap. A momentary gap where the ULTRA gang stopped flying at me. I knew I wasn't strong enough to disappear right now. But at least I could teleport the Failsafe somewhere else. Somewhere no one would ever find it.

And when I did, what happened to me... well, it happened.

As long as the Failsafe didn't get into the wrong hands. That was the main thing right now.

I went to lift the Failsafe out of my pocket and send it through a wormhole.

Before I could, someone snatched it from my grip.

I looked up and saw the fat ULTRA gurning with awe as he held onto the Failsafe. The rest of his people looked on in amazement, too, not believing what they were actually looking at.

"Thank you," Fat Morgan said. "Seriously. Thank you for this."

"Give it back here!"

"Oh, no. We can't do that. However, I'm starting to think maybe we could keep you close to your precious little metal ball of power."

He nodded, and before I understood why, I felt something tight and burning snap around my wrists. When I tried to use my abilities, my body surged with electricity. I was trapped.

"The Failsafe is worth a lot. A hell of a lot. But a Failsafe *and* Glacies? A Glacies with abilities? Hell, I might just be the most powerful dude ever to have lived."

I tried to break free of the ties again, but the electricity fought back even harder than I could give.

He had the Failsafe.

He had me.

I was his prisoner now.

18

I leaned back against the cell wall and wished I was anywhere but here.

It was dark. Cold. Miserable. I had no idea where I was, not really, or what time of day it was. I didn't think I'd traveled all that far when Fat Morgan and his band of misfits caught me. But maybe that was just the effect of the anti-energy bands around my arms, making me dizzy and nauseous every single time I tried to use my powers and break away from them.

Now here I was, trapped in a cell barely big enough to stretch out in.

There were bars to my left and right, but I didn't want to risk sticking my hands or legs through any of them because of the strange noises I'd heard. I squinted into the darkness, being careful not to activate my night vision so as to avoid another nasty shock. It was clear to me now that this was some kind of ULTRA prison. I wasn't sure exactly what Fat Morgan did with his ULTRAs when he had them here. Either he sold them off for financial gain or kept them as his pets. I wasn't sure.

I just knew that he had the Failsafe, and I didn't trust him with it.

I felt my stomach lurch with hunger, but at the same time, a wave of nausea covered me. In front of me, in the darkness, I saw something creeping around on the hard, damp floor, and I knew it was a rat. I held my breath when I saw it creeping past, more of them following. I'd never been keen on rats. They always gave me the creeps. Unlike most people with rat phobias, it wasn't the tail that bothered me so much. More that greasy fur of theirs. There was something sickening about it, imagining all the germs and badness embedded in that hair... It gave me the shivers. One time when I was younger, a rat had gotten into my bedroom. Rats were pretty common in New York, so it wasn't all that surprising.

I just remember waking up and feeling something crawling across my chest in the dark. At first, I thought it was Cassie playing around, teasing me.

Then I looked over at her bed and realized she was still there.

It was then that the rat started nibbling at my neck.

I'd screamed. I don't think I stopped screaming for hours. I didn't sleep in that bedroom again, one of the reasons why I ended up getting the room that Cassie had wanted to upgrade to herself all along.

I just remembered Mom holding me and telling me everything was going to be okay. That it couldn't get me anymore.

And as much as I wanted to believe her, as much as her presence reassured me, I still never felt secure around them. Like they were working their way up to that fateful day where they finally got their ratty revenge once and for all.

I saw them pass by and I swallowed a lump in my throat, letting myself breathe normally. Truth be told, I didn't know what to do. Part of me wanted to get out of this place and get the Failsafe back. But at the same time, that temptation to just sit back and not be a hero anymore was strong.

I felt guilty for even feeling slightly that way. But it was what it was.

I was about to close my eyes when something caught my attention to my right.

The guy in the cell was right up to the bars.

I lurched to my left. Instinctively I activated my powers, which gave me a nasty searing jolt.

But when my eyes focused, when I realized who was at the bars of that cell, I felt even more alarmed.

"Hello, Kyle. Fancy seeing you here."

He was gaunt. His face was bruised. He looked like an extra-skinny version of the guy I used to know, the guy I used to fight alongside.

But there was no doubting that smug grin.

It was Ember.

"What the hell are you doing in here?" I asked.

Ember didn't respond. Not at first. As a slither of moonlight peeked through the grating above the cells, I swore I saw tears building in his eyes. He didn't look like he'd spoken to anyone in a long time.

"Ember? How—"

"It really is you."

I closed my mouth and smiled as well as I could, considering the circumstances. "It really is."

"I never thought I'd see you again. Or anyone again. This place. It—it's mad. It makes you see things. You want to get out. You want to escape."

I heard a feverish intensity to Ember's voice like never before. I wondered how long he'd been here, and how long he'd taken to break.

"How did you end up stuck in here?"

"This group," Ember said. He shook his head, the smile shifting from his face. "These people. They trade. Trade in expensive things. ULTRAs as weapons. To gangs. To drug barons. Mikey said they brainwash us and ship us to fights in Japan. I don't wanna fight. Not anymore."

You and me both.

"What are you up to these days?" Ember asked, like it was the most casual crossing of paths in the world. "Still keeping people safe out there?"

I wanted to tell Ember I did. But I felt guilty lying. "I'm... There's not a lot of fighting to do anymore."

"Your choice?"

He'd seen right through my bullshit, then. "Something like that."

Ember didn't seem to judge, though. Just leaned back against the wall and tilted his head like he was weighing it up. "It's hard to keep fighting sometimes. But, hey. A lot of people rely on you. So you've got to keep going, no matter what."

I heard Ember's words and deep down, I knew he was right. I didn't like the idea people relied on me. But I knew it was the truth. And it made me feel even more shitty.

"Whatever you've done or not done or choose to do, there's one thing for sure. This place. You have to get out of here. Fast."

"I'm not sure I—"

"You can. You're strong enough. Always have been strong enough, even if you are a bit of a dick at times."

Ember laughed, and I did too. I felt like we were back how we used to be, back in the old days, the good days.

"So you ready to break out of here?"

I swallowed a lump and looked around at the dark, grim, cold, rat-infested hellhole. Ember was right. I had people relying on me. And right now that reliance came in the form of getting the Failsafe to safety.

"You know what?" I said. "I think I am."

19

Fat Morgan tucked into his fried chicken and by damn, it was the tastiest fried chicken he'd ever had in his life.

It was night, and he always liked to eat at night. Hell, he always liked to eat no matter what time of day it was. But nights were always the best. Especially the stormy ones. A day of trading and dealing out of the way and he'd settle down in his room with a whole host of snacks.

But this was the first bucket of chicken he'd treated himself to in weeks. And boy was he loving it.

He scraped his teeth against the bone of the chicken leg, the juicy, succulent fatty meat dribbling down his chin. He knew he was fat. He'd always been fat, right from when he was a kid. Dad used to tell him he was a fat little shit, but Mom always encouraged him to eat more and more. Dad said she had something wrong with her. That she had a kind of weird sick fantasy. Fat Morgan didn't know what that meant at the time, and sure, Mom did act weird a few times. Even got herself thrown in a mental hospital once or twice.

But she was just Mom. And Fat Morgan always loved her.

Right up until the day she just disappeared.

Which just made him want to eat more and more.

He chewed harder against the fried chicken and threw the bone, completely stripped of flesh, into the bucket. He looked around at this dark room he called home. It was basic. Any old prison was bound to be. Sure, it was rusty. And sure, there was a bit of a rat problem. But he kind of liked rats. They always used to be there for him when he was younger. He used to catch 'em. Stroke 'em. Raise 'em as pets. When he was taken away and put into foster care, times were tough. He didn't know who loved him or who he was supposed to love.

But he always had his pets. And they made him feel better, especially when it got really hard.

He put his bucket to one side and rubbed his fingers against his huge belly. He was sat on his favorite chair, and he didn't plan on moving all night. Especially not when there was a bottle of gin right in reach.

He grabbed the gin and let it slither down his throat, immediately feeling its buzz. He grinned and chuckled a little as he sipped. He wasn't going to be stuck here for long, anyway. Soon, he was gonna have a nice big mansion of his own. A fancy sports car or two. Loads of women.

He looked over at the Failsafe and smiled.

He was gonna live the dream. And Glacies and the Failsafe were gonna go a long way toward securing that.

He knew what he was planning was a risky move. After all, selling on Glacies and the Failsafe was no small feat. Glacies was powerful as hell, so brainwashing him was going to take time. And the Failsafe, well. He had to make sure he found the right buyer for that. The most trustworthy buyer. At the end of the day, the check mattered, but not if he sold it to some nut job who wasn't afraid to use it on a whim.

He had to meet his clients and he had to vet them. He had

to make sure—absolutely sure—they were the right people to sell to.

And when he did, then he'd get his mansion. Then he'd find his way outta this shithole. Then he'd be able to eat fried chicken to his heart's content.

Because he didn't *enjoy* doing what he did right now. No-sir. It was just a job. A way of putting food on the table. Or in the bucket.

Soon, that was gonna change.

He was getting his big break.

He was getting the rewards his hard work deserved—

A bang.

A massive bang against his door.

He frowned. Instantly, agitation crept through his body.

He told his people that they weren't to disturb him when the door was locked. Even put a Do Not Disturb sign on the door, which they always acknowledged. Always.

Except now.

'Cause the door banged some more.

Fat Morgan sighed and dragged his mass of weight from the chair. "Yeah, yeah. Coming. This better be good." He hadn't planned on moving all night. He was feeling pins and needles in his feet and toes, like they'd turned in for the evening too.

The door banged some more.

"I'm coming, alright? Give it a goddamned rest or I'll..."

When Fat Morgan opened the door, he got the feeling right away that this wasn't just any ordinary night.

In front of him was Bouncer. He could jump hella high.

He was covered in blood.

His hands were behind his back. He was shaking.

"What the hell's—"

"There's someone coming. An—an ULTRA."

"Just one damned ULTRA put you in this state?"

"It's—it's not my blood. But it will do. If we don't hand over the—the Failsafe."

Fat Morgan gritted his teeth. "That ain't gonna happen. Where is this idiot?"

"Morgan, seriously. He wants the Failsafe."

"Well he'd better pay really damned good."

"He isn't gonna pay."

Fat Morgan frowned. "What?"

"He—he said he isn't gonna pay." Bouncer started fumbling with something behind his back. "And—and he told me he wanted me to show you this. As—as proof."

"Show me what?"

Bouncer didn't have to answer.

He pulled the thing behind his back out and immediately Fat Morgan felt an iron rod of fear pierce through his chest.

In front of him was a head.

Root's head. Torn from his body.

Bouncer dropped the head to the floor, and it rolled into Fat Morgan's room. Fat Morgan would usually have gone mad at that. He would've reacted.

But then he saw the massive hooded figure stomping his way to him.

"What do we do?" Bouncer asked.

Fat Morgan gritted his teeth. He looked at the approaching figure, then he looked over his shoulder at the Failsafe.

"Morgan? What do we do?"

Fat Morgan took a deep breath.

Then he put a hand on Bouncer's shoulder.

"I'm sorry," he said.

Bouncer didn't have time to understand what Fat Morgan was apologizing about.

Fat Morgan smacked both hands and sent Bouncer flying into the oncoming assailant.

Fat Morgan didn't stick around to see how the figure reacted. He didn't wait to see whether Bouncer survived, or whether he even hit the figure.

He just turned around and flew at the Failsafe.

He grabbed it. And at that point, he did look over his shoulder.

When he did, he saw that the figure was close. So close.

And there was blood on his black cloak.

Bouncer's blood, surely.

"You ain't getting your dirty hands on this," Fat Morgan said, slipping the Failsafe into his pocket. "Not a goddamned chance."

The figure didn't do anything. Not at first.

And then he lifted a hand and some weird, swirly energy started appearing in front of it, spinning faster and faster.

Fat Morgan wanted to stay and fight for his people. He wanted to protect the ULTRAs—the valuable ULTRAs, like Glacies—who he had in those cells.

But the Failsafe was way more important.

The Failsafe was going to make him a rich man, and he wanted to be a rich man more than anything.

He watched a surge of energy fly toward him from the ULTRA's hands.

Fat Morgan squeezed his eyes shut.

And he held onto the Failsafe.

Tightly.

20

I held my breath and readied myself to do what I had to do.

I knew it wasn't going to be easy breaking out of the bands that were wrapped around my wrists. I'd tried a few times, pretty damned hard too.

But Ember was right when he'd told me what I had to do. I didn't have to try *hard*. Any old schmuck could try *hard*.

I had to try harder than hard.

I was Kyle goddamned Peters. Glacies. The strongest ULTRA alive.

And I wasn't going to let a bunch of lowlife bounty hunters dictate my life.

I squeezed my eyes shut and focused on the bubble of power I felt in the center of my chest.

Right away, I felt a kickback. Electricity burned up my arms, down my back, into my pelvis and through my legs.

I tensed my jaw and groaned as the agony stretched up the back of my neck, making the hairs on my head rise on end.

I couldn't see because my eyes were closed, but I could feel the pressure underneath my eyelids growing. I had a horrible image of my eyes bursting, leaving me totally blind. Then, I'd be screwed. Well and truly screwed.

I had to work hard to make sure that didn't happen.

I felt the electricity growing overwhelming and I knew I didn't have long left to fight. My energy was waning. Soon, I'd be dead.

Then I heard Ember's voice.

"Keep on pushing, Kyle. You can do this. You can do this..."

His voice faded away, but somehow I knew he was still speaking. I could feel his words moving through my body, giving me the strength to keep on pushing, to keep on fighting. It wasn't easy. It was the hardest damned thing I'd ever done. Okay, maybe a slight exaggeration. Not the hardest thing I'd ever done. But definitely up there.

Still I pushed back against that electricity.

Because I was going to get to the Failsafe.

And I was going to finish what I'd started.

I was going to—

I heard a blast in my skull.

Every muscle in my body went limp.

I wasn't sure how long I lay on the floor, stretched out. I was looking up at the ceiling; I knew that much. I couldn't hear properly. I could taste blood.

But I was alive.

The electricity might've hurt me, stopped me moving out of the cell, but I was...

When I lifted my head slightly, I realized I wasn't inside my cell anymore.

The anti-energy bands were inside my cell. They were lying on the floor, smoke rising from them.

Ember grinned and gripped onto the front bars of his cell. "Now go on. Go do what you have to do."

I didn't want to leave Ember behind. I felt so guilty about it. But it wasn't for good. "I'll be back for you. I swear."

"Just go," Ember said. He was smiling. And it wasn't a fake smile, either. He looked truly happy, truly relieved, to see me escape that cell. "Don't worry about me. I'm fine in here."

I turned toward the steps at the end of the corridor and I ran right up them.

I activated my invisibility, but I still felt like I was being watched, as empty as these corridors were. I couldn't believe how silent the place was. I swore I'd heard voices earlier, a constant movement.

When I reached the end of the corridor, I saw why.

There was blood on the walls.

And on the floor beside those walls, there were bodies.

I looked away, the smell triggering my gag reflex. I didn't want to look. Something had gone down here. Something big.

And a niggling feeling inside me told me it was probably to do with the Failsafe.

I walked through the door at the end of this corridor, which was ajar.

Inside, I saw a chair, which had a massive hole in it where someone clearly sat quite regularly. There was a bucket of chicken—well, *once* chicken, now bones—by the side of that chair. A smashed gin bottle lined the floor.

On the door, "Fat Morgan. Do Not Disturb."

This was where the leader of this place, Fat Morgan, lived.

But there was no sign of the Failsafe.

I searched the room, growing more and more agitated, more and more frustrated. I knew I wasn't going to find anything. Fat Morgan had fled, and of course he'd taken the Failsafe with him. I was going to have to go after him. I was...

When I turned around, I saw a dark figure standing in front of the doorway.

Catalyst.

He lifted his hands and went to fire a wave of energy at me.

I teleported myself out of the way of that blast and back down into the cells. Before I knew it, I was standing opposite Ember.

"Did you do it?" Ember asked, dragging his face closer to the cell. "Did you get what you wanted?"

"Ember, I—"

A blast opened up the door at the top of the corridor, knocking me to my ass. When I got back to my feet, I saw that Catalyst was just meters away.

"Go, Kyle," Ember said. He was lying down now, too. "Leave. Get out of here."

I shook my head. "I can't leave you."

"What you're chasing down is more important than me. It's more damned important than any of us. Just go. I'll let you off. This once. But I'll kick your ass when I see you again. That's a promise."

Ember smiled and laughed, but I could hear the sadness in his voice.

Catalyst stepped over me.

"I'm sorry," I said, as tears filled my eyes. I wanted to teleport Ember away too, but he still had bands on his arms. And I wasn't sure I had enough time. "I—"

"Just go."

"Ember. I'm so sorry."

He half-smiled, and for a moment, I saw total terror in his eyes as Catalyst went to blast me with his shockwaves.

And then I let out a cry and I teleported far away from this place with the last of the strength I had.

21

Catalyst walked down past the cell blocks and felt the anger burning up inside.

He listened to his footsteps tapping against the metal floor beneath. The air was thick with the smell of sweat and other bodily fluids. He could hear whimpering; the pained whimpers of people who had been trapped down here in this place for a long, long time. He didn't know their stories. He didn't know their pasts, and he didn't know whether they deserved to be here.

He just knew he was angry. Very angry.

He'd let the Failsafe slip again. He'd let that ULTRA slip, again.

He knew it was the same ULTRA he'd encountered over in Australia. He could smell it. Something about the way he perspired gave away his identity.

He didn't know who he was, exactly, but he was starting to wonder. Starting to question whether it was possible, all along.

He heard that niggling voice whispering in his ear as he carried on walking.

You're not good enough.

Failed again, like you always fail.

And he'd believed it. Catalyst had really believed he was weak, just like the voice in his head used to always tell him.

But now he was strong. He'd spent time training. Working hard to get to the stage he was at. He knew about the Failsafe, and he was going to track it down and use it. That was always the plan. He was strong enough to get that far. It was the goal, and it wasn't supposed to be this difficult.

He didn't account for the mystery ULTRA standing up to him. The one making it difficult for him.

He'd find out who he was, for certain.

And he'd kill him.

He kept on walking alongside the cells until he reached the one that was empty. He knew it was empty because he could feel his feet echoing against the wall at the back.

He could smell the presence of the mystery ULTRA, too.

This was his cell.

And there was someone in the cell next to where he'd been.

"You," Catalyst said.

He couldn't see the reaction of the person in the cell next door, but he could tell from the subtle change in temperature in the air that whoever was in that cell was worried. "Me?"

"The ULTRA in this cell. Who was it?"

Again, another subtle shift in the air temperature. And a long enough hesitation in speech for Catalyst to know that whatever was coming next was most likely a lie. "I don't know who the hell he was. And I wouldn't tell you if I did."

Catalyst smiled.

Then he lifted a hand, magnetically dragged the prisoner toward the cell bars and slammed his face and body right up against them.

"I'll ask you one more time," Catalyst said. He could detect real warmth about this ULTRA in particular. And he got the sense that, if allowed to use his powers, he'd be able to go up in flames. Fire was bubbling under his skin. Just a good job he had bands wrapped around his wrists, then. "And this time I suggest you answer. Who was in the cell?"

Resistance in the air. A struggle, as the prisoner choked, Catalyst pulling him even harder against the cell bars. "I... don't..."

"You think this is some kind of game?"

"I... I think you're—you're desperate. And there's nothing... nothing you can do to make me give up what I know."

Catalyst pulled the prisoner even harder against the cell bars and imagined all the horrible things he could do to change this stubborn bastard's mind. "Are you sure about that?"

He tightened his grip on the prisoner's arm and got ready to yank it from its socket.

"It was Glacies."

The voice came from the cell to the right of the empty one. And when Catalyst heard it, he dropped the prisoner right away and walked toward that cell. "What did you just say?"

There was silence for a few seconds. But there was no shift in the air. There was no panic. Just pure calm. Honesty. "Glacies," the voice repeated. "Kyle Peters. That was him in here just then."

Catalyst knew the name. He knew the legend. Everyone did. Kyle Peters was a big part of culture and society these days. He was a celebrity, in a way.

He was strong. He was powerful. He'd done some good things for the world.

But he'd supposedly lost his abilities.

Which made things interesting.

Very interesting.

Catalyst looked at where he knew the prisoner was standing. And then he turned and looked back at the other prisoner. The stubborn one.

He walked over to the front of his cell. He stood there for a few seconds, just listening to his heartbeat, feeling the fear that bubbled under his skin no matter how hard he tried to prove he wasn't afraid.

"You're lucky I just got the information I wanted," Catalyst said. "For that, I'll make this next part a lot less painful."

Then he slammed the prisoner against the bars once more, hard enough to knock all consciousness from his body.

He heard every bone crack, and then a thud, as the body of the ULTRA hit the cell floor.

"Sleep tight."

He turned around and walked to the cell doors.

"Wait," someone shouted. The man who'd given up Glacies' identity. "What about me? Not gonna let me outta here?"

Catalyst turned around and looked at the prisoner's cell. "Thank you. Sincerely. But now you must serve your time."

"Hey! You bastard! You let me outta here! You let me go!"

Catalyst turned away and climbed the steps toward the cell doors as the man's shouting continued to echo around this hellhole.

He knew what he had to do.

He knew who he was up against.

And he was going to stop him reaching that Failsafe, no matter what it took.

22

I flew away from Fat Morgan's prison as quickly as I could, but in all honesty, I didn't have a clue where I was heading.

It was light now, which was disorienting, as I'd been plunged into near darkness for God knows how long. My lips were dry and chapped, and my stomach was calling out with hunger. I still hadn't found a chance to take a break. I was too eager to get away from Catalyst.

But more than that, I was too eager to chase down Fat Morgan and get to the Failsafe.

As I flew through the sky, no real sense of direction or purpose, I thought about my family and friends back home. They'd be worried now, surely. At least I hoped they would be, goddammit. They'd see by now that something was amiss and they'd be concerned. As much as I didn't want them to think anything bad had happened to me, I couldn't talk to them. I had another duty right now, as painful as it was, and as reluctant as I was to pursue it.

I thought about the last time I'd been home. I'd been in that arcade with Damon and Avi. I'd gone to the bathroom and got surrounded by those mysterious people, who turned out to be working for Michael Williamson. They'd have been worried right away. They'd probably start asking questions like how could I just disappear like that.

I knew that wherever Cassie is, she'd be cautiously optimistic about all this. She'd maybe believe that I was embracing my powers and abilities again.

And, sure. I wouldn't go as far as saying I was *embracing* them. That's a little too strong a word to describe my attitude to my newly re-discovered hero status. But I was using them. And I was going to keep on using them until I found that Failsafe.

And then, when I'd finally put all this shit to bed, I'd hang my costume up for good.

Or burn it. Probably a more permanent solution.

But for now, I had to keep going. And the more I moved, the more I realized how aimless this was. If I wanted to find where Fat Morgan had gone, I needed to go back to where they'd gone *from* and find some kind of trace. Some kind of clue.

Of course, being an ULTRA, that didn't exactly mean I had to *physically* go back.

I closed my eyes while I hovered in the sky and took myself back to Fat Morgan's office. I looked around it. Looked at where the Failsafe had been. Looked at the notes scattered across his desk. Looked at the indentation in his chair, where his fat ass had dug a hole. I looked at the magazine on the floor.

Nothing.

I gritted my teeth as I continued to struggle. There had to be something. Some kind of clue or other. A place like that couldn't just be empty of clues or evidence. It wasn't possible.

I started to consider that maybe actually physically returning to the place was a good idea.

And then I heard the voice in my head.

"We go to the base in the Darien Gap," it said. "Anything

goes to shit, that's where we go. We lay low there for two weeks near the jungle and we don't say a word to anyone else. Okay? There's guards there. There's troops there. Tough mother-f-ers. They'll keep us safe. Help us lay low. Right?"

The voice was muffled, and I couldn't recall when I'd heard those words uttered the first time. But I knew I must've taken it in when I was sitting in that cell ready to give in.

Darien Gap.

A base in the jungle.

That vastly narrowed down my search radius.

Before I returned to reality, I had to look at the cells. I had to know Ember was okay. I didn't know what'd happened to him, and a part of me didn't even want to find out.

But I had to see.

I followed my consciousness, my physical body still else-where, down those steps toward the cells.

I saw the prisoner that had been in the cell beside me holding onto the bars, shaking them.

I saw the cell I'd been stuck inside.

And then the one…

When I looked inside Ember's cell, I flashed right back to my physical self.

My teeth chattered. My body shook.

Ember wasn't there anymore.

But his cell was filled with blood.

I immediately teleported over to the Darien Gap, the border between Colombia and Panama, and was hit with a wave of humidity. I felt dizzy, too, like my powers were taking it out of me more than they used to. Besides, this place wasn't exactly safe. The most dangerous place in the world, apparently.

I headed over to the jungles, across the Darien Gap, searching for hours. I flew through them, searching, just eager to find some sign of a compound, some sign of…

I saw it, then.

Movement.

Movement between the trees.

An ULTRA, down there on the ground.

Fat Morgan. No doubt about it.

I flew down toward him. I knew he had the Failsafe. And I knew I had to take it off him.

I crept through the air as slowly and stealthily as I could.

Then he turned around.

Even though I was invisible—at least I was certain I was invisible—he looked right into my eyes and shook his head. "Shoulda stayed far away from here, kid."

I tensed my fists and readied to fire a blast of ice at him.

But before I could, he lifted his hands and threw me back into the sky telekinetically.

I slammed into a tree, cracking the back of my head against the bark.

I tumbled down toward the ground, rapidly losing consciousness.

And as much as I tried to use my abilities to ease my fall, I couldn't.

They weren't working.

I wasn't strong enough.

And I was falling. Rapidly.

23

I regained my composure, held my breath, and twisted around in the air so I was facing Fat Morgan.

He wasn't there anymore. He'd run inside.

But I wasn't alone.

I felt the blasts of anti-energy surge toward my body, and I knew right then I was in for a fight.

Again.

Hey. I was retrieving a Failsafe that had the power to shut down every darned ULTRA on the planet. I couldn't exactly expect the thing to be weakly guarded.

I spun to my right, swerving out of the way of an anti-energy blast. Then another one came flying at me, and I had to teleport just out of its reach.

I scanned my surroundings then. Beneath me, I realized there were four of those guards. They didn't look like ULTRAs, which did me a favor in the long run. I figured Fat Morgan must've kept this little metal building under wraps as a kind of safe place in case of emergency and had guards right on call.

Well he was lucky it was me who'd arrived and not Catalyst. I might just be a little more lenient.

In that I'd try my best not to kill everybody in this darned compound.

Out of nowhere, another anti-energy blast surged at my face. And another, right to the middle of my chest.

They were flying at me too fast.

I couldn't dodge them both. Not with more of those blasts circling me.

So I closed my eyes and followed my instincts.

Those instincts took me down to the ground. Right behind two of those guards.

I tapped one on the shoulder as he looked around, baffled at where I'd gone.

"Boo," I said.

I slammed my hands against him and immediately opened up a wormhole right behind his friend.

He went crashing into his friend, and the pair of them slipped into that wormhole and vanished. They'd wake up, somewhere. I wasn't killing them. Just giving them a little punishment for poor life choices.

They'd learn from their mistakes.

And if they didn't, well. Maybe next time I wouldn't be so lenient.

I felt something sting my back and I knew I'd been hit. But instinctively, I spun around and dragged the surge from my flesh before it could sink any deeper. I threw it back at the two guys firing at me. They sizzled with the blast, smoke rising from their bodies.

I thought about leaving them there. They'd hurt me, after all. And I didn't like people who hurt me. Not one bit.

But I couldn't help feeling a twinge of sympathy for them. They were only doing their jobs.

So I clicked my fingers, dulling the impact of the electricity in an instant, and then sent those to the other side of the world to join their buddies in a new life.

Then, I turned around and faced the building.

It was a small place. Easy enough to miss. Like a big metal hatch covered in grass and weeds. All around me, I heard the sounds of the jungle. I didn't want to stay out here too long and risk coming face to face with anything nasty, so I made a break for the door.

To my surprise, the door opened easily. Not much like the hatch out of Lost that it looked like at first glance after all. I made my way through the dusty corridors, the smell of rusty metal strong in the air.

As my footsteps echoed against the metal, I swore I could hear somebody else. I wasn't sure where from, but you know that feeling you get when you're being watched? Well I got that. And being Glacies, I got it to the extreme.

That feeling was tingling like mad right now.

I kept on walking, though, picking up my pace, keeping invisible just in case I came across anyone. I looked behind every single door, even the ones with massive locks, but nothing.

Not until I reached the fourth door from the end on the right.

When I went in there, I saw exactly what I'd come for.

It was the Failsafe. It looked a little less shiny, like it'd been through a lot. Which it had, really.

But it was here. So I had to get it and I had to take it back.

I lunged for it. Went to pick it up.

The Failsafe didn't move.

I frowned. There was something wrong about this. The Failsafe was stuck. It was wedged in. It was...

At that point, I realized I wasn't holding the Failsafe at all.

I heard footsteps behind me.

I looked back.

Fat Morgan was standing opposite me.

He was holding onto the Failsafe.

"One false move and I'll switch this thing on and wipe out the both of us," he said.

24

I watched as Fat Morgan held onto the Failsafe—the *real* Failsafe—and threatened to push the button that would put the pair of us out of existence.

Well. Not push a button exactly. There was no button on that thing that I could see. But... do whatever he had to do. Whatever that was.

Shit. I really should've done my homework. Would've appreciated a lesson or two from Michael Williamson on how the Failsafe actually worked before going after it. I didn't exactly want to accidentally sit on it and blow everyone up. That wouldn't exactly be the smoothest of moves.

Fat Morgan's eyes looked bloodshot and transfixed. Other than his breathing, there was total silence in this hideout of his. I could smell his sweat, and I knew he was terrified. Terrified of what might happen if he lost the Failsafe. Of the power it would strip away from him.

"You killed my men," he said. "That wasn't a good move."

"I didn't kill your men, for what it's worth. As for whether it's a good move or not, well. I'm here now."

"And you're gonna regret ever setting foot in here."

"I'll believe that when I see it. But let's get one thing straight right now. Only one of us is leaving this place with the Failsafe. And I'm going to do everything in my power to make sure that's me."

A smile stretched across Fat Morgan's face. "Y'know, all my life I've had to deal with people tellin' me I'm not good enough. All my life I've had to put up with people *taking* and *taking* and *taking*. But enough's enough. There ain't gonna be no more taking. Not from me. Not if it kills me. So you're gonna turn around and get your weak ass outta here, or you're gonna kill the both of us. You were wrong when you said just one of us is gettin' outta here. Very wrong. It's either me or none of us. Take it or leave it."

I thought about zooming over there and snatching the Failsafe from Fat Morgan's grip. But I knew it was too risky. The way he was talking, it was like a man who'd lost everything. Who was making the biggest gamble of all. Playing a lethal game of Russian Roulette that he hoped was going to work in his favor.

"I'll give you ten seconds to get your ass outta here or I'll—"

"That Failsafe. It's... It's important that it doesn't self-destruct because there's people out there I care about. ULTRAs. Good ULTRAs. You have to know good ULTRAs too. Ones you don't want to see fall. Surely you can see that?"

Fat Morgan's eyes narrowed. "There ain't no ULTRAs I care about. And I don't give a rat's ass what *you* care about either. All I care about is my mansion. My future. All I care about is sitting on the sofa and eating chicken wings without a worry in the world."

"And if you detonate that Failsafe, you are never going to see that life."

"And if I don't, what? You're just gonna walk away with it, and I ain't ever gonna see that life either."

I swallowed a lump in my throat. "Not—not necessarily."

I saw Fat Morgan's eyes narrow as he tried to understand what I was implying.

"You hand that Failsafe over and I'll return it to safety. As soon as I do, I'll... You can take me. Take me as prisoner. Sell me to the highest bidder."

Fat Morgan started to smile. Then he chuckled. "You'd do that, would you?"

"Yes."

"You'd really give it all up just to keep our kind alive?"

"My sister is an ULTRA. I have friends who are ULTRAs. If it's a choice between a life of captivity or a life without them, I know which option I'd choose every time."

There was silence between us. No sounds but the tropical birds outside. The heaviness of Fat Morgan's breathing.

"Hand it over. Please. I don't want this to get ugly."

Fat Morgan looked down at the Failsafe. His face started to soften.

Then he looked back up at me and smiled. "'Fraid it's already gonna get ugly, kid."

He twisted the Failsafe.

I closed my eyes and waited for non-existence or whatever awaited to occur.

I saw a bright light surging out of the Failsafe.

I waited for it to cover my body, to tear me apart...

But nothing happened.

Nothing at all.

The pair of us stood there, frowning. Fat Morgan held the Failsafe in his shaking hand, his eyes transfixed by the beauty of the thing he was holding.

He looked up at me, and for a second, I saw realization in his eyes. Realization that his plan hadn't worked. Realization that he didn't even know how to activate this thing at all.

I was about to fly toward him and grab the Failsafe when I heard a bang on the roof, and then Fat Morgan was no more.

It took me a few seconds to understand what I'd just witnessed, as I tumbled back onto my ass. My head spun. My ears rang with the shockwaves.

I lifted myself up and I saw exactly what had happened.

Catalyst was here.

He had crashed through the roof and landed right on top of... well, what was once Fat Morgan. The less description about his current violent state, the better. Just safe to assume he wouldn't be eating any more fried chicken anytime soon.

And in Catalyst's hand, the Failsafe.

He looked at me. Tilted his head.

"I'll deal with you, in time. But for now, I have somewhere I need to be."

I tensed my fists and ice covered them.

I lifted my hands and fired at Catalyst.

The ice just stopped in thin air.

Then it turned back to me, pointed in my direction.

"You're weak, now. Which is why you aren't an immediate concern. But I promise you, I'll deal with you. I have to hurry. More important matters at hand. Watch your step. Glacies."

My ice blasted back toward me and hit me right in the chest.

I fell back with violent force, cracking my head, my back, everything on the ground.

I struggled to get back up. Tried to re-activate my abilities. Did all I could to spring myself back to life.

But it was too late.

Catalyst was gone.

The Failsafe was gone.

25

I sat on a rocky slope in the middle of the Australian Outback and sipped back an icy cold Coca-Cola, imagining my problems were non-existent.

Of course, I could only trick myself for so long. Reality had a funny way of catching up like that.

I looked across the vast expanse of barren land at the setting sun. It was glowing orange, the sandy ground simmering with the heat. I knew we were only just getting to the end of Australian winter, but their winters were something special compared to the ones I got back home. There was no sign of snow in sight, for one. Which was convenient. I spent enough time with icy hands as it was. Didn't need a load of snow to remind me of who I really was, deep down.

The silence was what brought me here more than anything. Total silence. Total lifelessness. I really felt like I could hide out here forever, alone with my thoughts, and nobody would find me. And that'd be totally fine because it meant I didn't have to *be* anyone else just to satisfy others anymore. It meant I could just be myself.

And I wanted nothing more than to be myself. Power-free.

I looked to my right and saw the space where Daniel had sat not all that long ago. We'd sat on the top of this slope and discussed the way things were going, Daniel sipping a beer. He'd told me that I needed to watch my step. That I needed to focus, now more than ever, because something big and bad was coming. And although I knew things were different now—although circumstances had changed—I still heard Daniel's words as clear as I'd heard them that day back then.

Only he wasn't here to guide me anymore.

Weird thought, really. The idea of being *guided* by someone like Nycto. Someone I thought I hated, once. Someone I'd fought against, who I'd put at the bottom of a volcano in the hope he never resurfaced.

Really, such a short amount of time had passed. And yet so much had changed in that space of time.

I wished Daniel was here right now to talk to again. I wished he were here to consult. Sure, he was no angel, but he was clever. Cleverer than me, probably.

But I was alone right now.

I was alone, and Catalyst had the Failsafe.

Just thinking about Catalyst holding on to the Failsafe made my skin crawl. He was dangerous. Very dangerous. And I had no doubt about his intentions to use that Failsafe, even if it meant his own destruction. Or if he didn't use it *literally*, he'd still use it as an object to lead a reign of fear over everyone beneath him. There were so many ULTRAs in the world now. They made up a percentage of the population. A very small percentage in the grand scheme of things—in the thousands—but they were a significant enough group to worry about the consequences of someone dangerous like Catalyst threatening them.

Or using fear to turn them into his very own army, for whatever reason.

All of the possibilities terrified me.

Besides. My sister was an ULTRA. And even Damon had absorbed—and lost—ULTRA abilities. I couldn't put any of them at risk. I couldn't allow anything to happen.

I put my face in my hands and squeezed my eyes shut. I was hungry, but my appetite was crowded out by the nerves I had over the inevitability of the situation I was in. I was at a crossroads. A crossroads between sinking back into that life of running away from who I was, from all my responsibilities as a hero—and another road—a road where I embraced who I was now. Where I stopped running away from my fears and started truly chasing my goal.

It might mean sacrificing my life as Kyle Peters, human, once and for all.

But if I didn't do anything, then it'd mean sacrificing my life —and the lives of all the ULTRAs in the world—in the process.

I pulled my head out of my hands, took a deep breath, and stood up.

I stared over the edge of the cliff and looked at the sun as it got closer to the horizon. I didn't know why the Failsafe didn't work when Fat Morgan tried to use it. I didn't know whether he'd even activated it properly at all. Come to think of it, perhaps he just didn't know how either. Perhaps no one did.

But regardless of anything, I wasn't willing to risk anyone dying.

Might be uncomfortable embracing who I was. But I would do. Even if it meant giving up my life as Kyle Peters for now, I'd have a chance to turn back to it later, when all this was done.

There were just no guarantees of that anymore. That was something I had to live with.

I looked up into the sky and I saw my future clearly, for the first time in a long while.

I *had* to be Glacies.

I *had* to embrace who I was.

I *had* to get that Failsafe back from Catalyst.

And I was going to do everything within my power to make sure that happened.

I closed my eyes, took in a deep breath, and felt a tingling sensation spread across my body.

Then I flew up into the sky and teleported out of here.

26

One week without contact and Michael Williamson was starting to get worried about Kyle Peters.

It was late at night, but it could've been any time of day down here in Michael's windowless, underground office. Apparently, it was a warm night, but again, his air conditioning in this place did a solid job of disguising any natural weather conditions on the outside and converting them to those of his preference. He leaned against the edge of his table. The table he ate his food at, at least twenty-five days a month. The table he'd spoken to Kyle Peters across just days ago.

He could sit down. He could make some food. He could go home and see his wife, Olive.

But he was worried about Kyle.

Especially after hearing the rumors.

A bitter taste crossed Michael's lips when he glanced toward his laptop. Talks of an ULTRA in Australia. An ULTRA with a strong telekinetic ability, as well as serious strength. He'd heard of this ULTRA several times over the years. He'd been biding his time, waiting in the background for his perfect moment to strike. And Michael knew exactly who this ULTRA was.

Catalyst.

Just thinking of the name made Michael's stomach ache. It put him right off the idea of food, for a long time for sure. Because he knew what Catalyst wanted. It went beyond the Failsafe. And there was a bittersweet reality to Catalyst finding that Failsafe. Mostly because Catalyst didn't truly realize just how powerful he would be making himself. Not fully.

He walked across the tiled floor, his footsteps echoing around this vast expanse of an office. He grabbed his phone and stood with it for a few seconds, unsure of whether to go ahead with the phone call. He wanted to make that call. No doubt about it. But at the same time, he was afraid. Because he feared if he made that call, it'd be the last time he ever spoke to her in his entire life.

He didn't want to face up to that reality.

But he called anyway.

He listened to the dialing tone. The longer it rang, the more agitated and uncertain he grew. How strange that two people who had once loved each other could find such distance between them. How tragic that two lovers were nothing more than strangers, now.

The dialing tone cut out, and Michael heard her voice. "Hello?"

Michael smiled the moment he heard it. Olive's voice had a soothing effect on him, making him feel like he was okay, and like all was well with the world. It'd been the same way since he'd met her three years ago, marrying her a year later. Sure, they were old. But when he spoke with Olive, he felt like he was young again. They both did. "Honey. It's me."

"Michael? I... I didn't expect you to... You know. When you're working."

"I've got some free time right now," Michael said, instantly feeling guilty about the reluctance in his wife's voice. "Look, I... I've made some mistakes over the years."

"What're you talking about?"

"But I promise you I'm gonna make those right. I'm gonna work my ass off to get things better again. Between us. I'm gonna make us as great as we used to be, back when we first met."

Michael heard a silence at the other end of the line. It was only when he tasted salt on his top lip that he realized he was crying. And judging by the silence, Olive was crying too.

"I miss you," she said.

"I'll be home soon. For good."

"I'll make you steak. Like I used to."

"With your bare hands?"

"You betcha. Best way to make it."

He was starting to lose himself in the fantasy when he heard a crack.

A crack, somewhere to his right.

He spun around. The noise was unusual in a place of such silence. There was nothing in here that could make such a sound. Unless a computer had blown or something. But that didn't seem likely.

"Olive, I've gotta go. I..."

His voice trailed off when he realized there was no one on the line.

He was alone. Totally alone.

Well. Not totally alone.

Because he had that niggling feeling creeping up his spine that someone else was in here with him.

He walked slowly over to the place where he'd heard the crack. He grabbed an anti-energy pistol from the table and held it in his shaking hand. He crept toward the source of the noise, heart racing, head spinning with all kinds of possibilities.

What if they'd come for him?

What if it was Catalyst?

What would it mean?

He reached the place where he'd heard the crack. A desk. The other side of the desk.

Michael held his breath and lifted his pistol. He was sure someone was there.

He gritted his teeth.

Went to step around the desk.

There was nobody there.

Just a computer mouse lying on the floor.

Michael swallowed a lump in his throat and sighed. He went down to pick the mouse up. It musta just fallen. Musta just slipped from the desk. That's all it was. He was just being paranoid. He was just...

When he got back to his feet, that sense that someone was in here was stronger than ever.

His fears were confirmed when he saw someone's reflection on the computer monitor.

He spun around and held up his anti-energy pistol, pulling the trigger.

He didn't get to pull the trigger.

His fingers cracked. Each and every one of them.

They twisted out of their sockets and snapped, like nothing more than twigs.

Michael let out a yelp and went to fall down to his knees.

Instead, he went crashing back into the glass wall, and he felt himself being pressed against it. Hard.

When his blurry vision cleared, he saw who was holding him up.

Not that it surprised him in any way.

The dark clothing.

The hood.

The covered face.

Catalyst.

Catalyst walked slowly to Michael. Every footstep was long and drawn out. The way he moved creeped Michael out. His silence scared him. Everything about Catalyst intimidated him.

Then, Catalyst stopped just a foot away from him, staring up into Michael's eyes from within the darkness of that hood.

"Remember me?" he asked.

Hearing him speak brought back all the memories of the terrible things Michael had been involved in. The horrible things he'd done. "Jason. I never meant to—"

"Don't say it," Catalyst said, reaching for his hood. "Don't you dare say you never meant to hurt me. And don't you *dare* call me Jason."

He pulled down his hood.

Michael looked away. He couldn't bear to see what he'd caused. He couldn't face the truth.

"You will look at me!"

Michael didn't have a choice. His neck snapped round and his eyelids stretched open.

He stared into the face of the monster he'd created.

Catalyst was pale and bald. He looked older than his mid twenties. There were purple patches on his head. His skin looked really thin and weak. All across his face, scars and lacerations.

But they weren't even the most distinguishing things about Catalyst.

The most distinguishing things were the holes where his eyes used to be, now completely covered over with skin.

"You put me through this because you wanted me to be your

little project. You trained me. Made me strong. But you put me through so much pain to get what you wanted."

"Catalyst, I—"

"How's it feel now the shoe is on the other foot? How does it feel now *you* are the experiment?"

"None of you. I never meant to—"

"Stop saying you never meant to hurt me. Because you did what you did. I know not every ULTRA is aware of the pain so many were put through to make them who they are, but I remember. I remember clearly. So now you will do as I say."

He lifted his hand, and Michael felt himself choking.

"The Source," Catalyst said, lifting the Failsafe out of his pocket. "The location where I activate the Failsafe. Where is it?"

Michael couldn't talk if he wanted to. Not with Catalyst's telekinetic grip so tight around his neck. He struggled for breath. Battled against it.

Then Catalyst loosened his grip.

Michael caught his breath. He panted, dizzy, colors filling his vision.

"Well?" Catalyst asked.

Michael swallowed a lump in his throat as the memories of what he'd put Catalyst through when he'd been working on more recent experiments of the Hero project filled his mind, haunted his thoughts. "I won't tell you. No matter what you put me through, I'll never tell you. Never."

A smile twitched at the corners of Catalyst's thin, chapped mouth.

"I'm glad you said that," he said.

All of a sudden, Michael felt intense pressure building.

Right behind his eyes.

"Because I want you to go through what I went through. Worse than I went through."

"Please—"

"And when we're finally finished, we'll see just how resistant you are."

Michael kicked out. He punched the wall. He did everything his aging old body could to battle free of Catalyst's grip.

But that pressure behind his eyes kept on building.

Kept on intensifying.

"Tell me."

"Never," Michael gasped.

Catalyst held his hand in midair. The pressure stabilized, just for a second.

Then he shifted his hand toward the right and pointed at Michael's left eye.

"Then we'll start with the left one."

"Plea—"

Michael might've finished shouting. He couldn't be sure.

Because he felt the most pain he'd ever felt in his life, and with that pain in his left eye socket, darkness replaced vision.

And the real sickener?

He knew the pain was only just getting started.

He thought of Olive and prayed he'd die quickly.

But deep down he knew his prayers weren't going to be answered this time.

27

When I returned home, Cassie was already waiting for me at the front door, like she'd been standing there ever since I went missing.

I walked up the steps toward my home and I felt guilt every time I glanced up at her. I could tell she'd been crying. She'd been worried about me. Which meant, no doubt, that everyone had been worried about me. And of course they had. I'd gone missing. I hadn't checked in at all. I'd vanished, left my family and friends wondering where I was at.

That said, I wasn't exactly expecting a slap around the face.

My cheek stung when Cassie's hand made contact with my cheek. Then she grabbed both sides of my face and made me look at her. "You don't do that."

"I was—"

"You don't get to just vanish without a goodbye and leave us like that. Especially not Dad. Not after what happened."

I knew what Cassie was referring to. Herself. All these years my family had been convinced Cassie had been taken away from them. Now, she was back. But then I'd gone and vanished, and that could only have made my dad feel terrible.

"I'm sorry," I said. "There were some things I... I needed to sort out."

"Well you'd better get your ass in that sitting room and you'd better have a darned good excuse. Or you'll be getting another slap across the face, pronto."

I went into the house with Cassie. She called Dad, told him I was fine, that I'd just been away for a few days. Kept it awfully vague, which I appreciated. I wasn't ready to be totally open about my powers just yet.

"So go on," Cassie said. "You're out with Damon and Avi and you just vanish. Then you turn up like, a week later looking like total shit. What gives?"

I shook my head. Part of me didn't want to face the problem of Catalyst and the Failsafe. But the other part of me was growing stronger. The part that wanted to make a plan. To get the Failsafe back and end this madness once and for all.

And I couldn't do it alone.

"Well?" Cassie said.

"There's a Failsafe."

"A what now?"

"A Failsafe," I said. "A guy called Michael Williamson created the ULTRAs years back. He was made to make a Failsafe, in case of disaster. He swore it was in a secret place that could never be found. But now it's out there. And it's in the hands of someone dangerous. Really dangerous."

I saw Cassie's eyes narrow, like she was unconvinced about this whole thing. "So, what, you witness an armed bank robbery and you stand there shitting your pants, but one whiff of a threat to yourself and you're galvanized back into action?"

"It's not about that, Cassie."

"Then what's it about?"

"I've made mistakes. I accept that. I can see I've screwed up. But right now, everyone's lives are at stake. Not just ULTRAs.

People, too. Catalyst's the kind of guy who won't have good intentions for anyone. And I've no doubt he's gonna use that thing, as soon as he figures a way. And if he doesn't, well. He'll have something planned. No doubt about that."

Cassie was silent for a few seconds. "So you've come back here, why?"

"I need your help."

"Oh," Cassie said, rolling her eyes. "*Now* you need my help."

"I'm sorry for what happened. I'm sorry for everything. I'm sorry for acting like a spoiled brat."

"That's a start."

"But now's not the time for messing around. We need to build a team. A team capable of taking on Catalyst. Because... because yeah, I'm strong. But I can't do this alone."

Cassie was quiet again for a while. Looked like she was really mulling over what I'd said.

Then, "Ellicia's gone to San Fran already, you know?"

Those words hit me like a dagger to the chest. "She's..."

"She left early. Figured you'd walked away from her so decided to make a clean break. I'm sorry. Really. But you did this. You have to see that."

I sighed. San Fran might just be a teleport away, but it still seemed like the other side of the world with Ellicia being that far away from me, meeting new people, mixing with new friends... and guys. "I'll fix things between us. I swear I will. But right now, getting that Failsafe is more important. So will you help me?"

The pause stretched on longer than was comfortable. I thought Cassie was about to turn me down.

Then she stepped toward me and put a hand on my shoulder. "Looks like we'd better get tracking our people down, huh?"

I smiled. For the first time in God knows how long, I actually smiled.

Then I saw movement in the corner of my eye.

I lifted my hand, covered it in ice, went to fire a blast at the figure at the back of the room.

Then I realized I didn't have to.

"Damon?" I said.

Damon looked sheepishly between Cassie and I. "Heard—heard what you were saying just then. About building a team."

"What the hell are you doing here?"

He looked down at the floor, his cheeks red. "There's somethin' I haven't been totally honest about."

I narrowed my eyes. "Damon?"

He looked up at me, then he pulled his hands out of his pockets.

Purple electricity moved across them both, lighting up the room.

28

"You could've been straight with me."

"Um, Kyle. *You* coulda been straight with *me*."

"I didn't want anyone to know I still had powers."

"So, what? Things got a little tough and you opted out or something?"

"It wasn't like that. Anyway, you can hardly talk."

"Huh?"

"I mean, you kept your powers a secret. You're hardly one to judge."

"Yeah, but I'm not Glacies. I'm not the world's most powerful ULTRA. I don't have responsibilities like you do."

"Fair point."

"Yeah it is a fair point. So what're you gonna do about it?"

I swallowed the lump in my throat as I sat at the table across from Damon. It felt like we were spilling it all out. The truth. Our secrets. Everything we'd been hiding. I couldn't lie, there had been a kind of distance formed between us since the incident with Daniel, where Damon had effectively betrayed me and stood against me once Adam gave him his abilities. And this bit of dishonesty didn't exactly go a long way toward reassuring each other that it was all cards on the table.

But we were getting there. Slowly but surely.

"I'm guessing that's why you got captured in the first place," Damon said.

"What?"

"In the arcade. I'm guessing you got captured 'cause of your abilities."

"I was given a job. That job was to retrieve something important."

"Kyle, man, you don't have to dumb things down to me. Not anymore. I want to understand. I want to help."

I shook my head. "It's too dangerous, Damon. The world I fight in. It's too big and messy for you to get involved."

"You don't get to decide that."

"I—"

"No, Kyle. Just because you want to be the only one of your friends with abilities, I'm sorry. You don't have like, a God-given right anymore to make those kinds of decisions. I am who I am. I tried to hide it. I can't anymore. And I want to do something with what I've got. Something... something good."

I put my hand on Damon's shoulder. "What happened. To Daniel. That wasn't—"

"I'm not doing this just 'cause of Daniel," Damon snapped. "I'm doing it 'cause of *me*. I have abilities. I can't just leave them to rot while you and whoever goes searching for this Failsafe. I'm not hiding anymore. I'm not running away from who I really am. This is me. Damon. Although... I'd better get myself a hero name, right?"

I sniggered a little and shook my head. "We've come a long way."

"And we'll keep on going. Just things will be, well, a little different now."

"Just a little."

"Are you sure about this?" I asked.

I looked into Damon's eyes and tried to find a glimmer of uncertainty. Just enough to give me the ammunition to fight against him.

But I saw nothing but certainty.

"I want to help. I want to do something good with my life. And this is it."

I half-smiled, unable to contain the slight disappointment I felt. Only because I cared, though. Only because I worried about losing my best friend. I wasn't sure I could bear losing anyone else. "You'd better tell Avi why you aren't hanging around with him as much for the next while then."

"Oh, don't worry about Avi. He just picked up the sequel to that book he's always going on about. No doubt he'll be swimming in babes by the time he hits the end of the first chapter."

We both laughed. And when we laughed, it was like the old versions of ourselves laughing. No secrets. Everything out in the open. No lies. Nothing between us.

"So where do we start?" Damon asked.

I looked over at the door and saw Cassie standing there, smiling.

"I think I know exactly where to start," she said. "And where to find him."

S tone sipped back his umpteenth beer and forgot what it felt like to be sober.

It was late. Hell, it didn't really matter what time it was. Every day was the same these days. Wake up, do a few little chores around the house, then go to the nearest bar and drink. If anyone recognized him in that bar, he'd up sticks and move to another town where they didn't recognize him.

Until they did. And then the cycle would start all over again.

He squinted out of the window beside him. He could see specks of rain hitting the thin panes of glass and hear the wind rattling outside as the ocean picked up in intensity. He'd heard something about a storm being mentioned. Some nasty storm that was going to take the Indonesian island of Lombok by, well, storm. He'd been warned to get out of this place. To find somewhere to shelter for the night, preferably off the island if he wanted to secure his own safety.

But Stone didn't give a shit about his own safety. Not anymore.

Besides. He was made of rock. He could handle a bit of wind.

He looked around the bar, his eyes barely focusing on everything in his wake. There were a couple of people in here still. A few old-timers, who were too stubborn to make a move. He'd look out for them if he had to. But hell. He didn't realize how drunk he actually was. Drunk enough that when he looked to the left, it took his right eye a second to catch up. Maybe a storm would do him good after all. Slap him around a little, make him more conscious.

He heard the rattling glass getting louder, the wind shaking the building he was inside. The lights above flickered, and the crappy old static television in the corner above the bar flickered, then finally cut out. A few grumbles of discontent carried around the bar. Well, what the hell did these folks expect? Should've stayed at home. They weren't as tough as him. Weren't anywhere near as strong.

Anyway, he could do with some peace and quiet.

Even if he was feeling a bit queasy, the beer bitter against his tongue.

Honestly, this was pretty much how Stone's life had gone since the Resistance had disbanded. There'd been discussions of bringing the team together soon after Adam's defeat. But it ended up just not being feasible. The old Resistance wasn't the same. There was too much baggage attached to it. The world needed a new poster force now there were tons more ULTRAs floating about. A new team to make them behave, keep them in check.

Besides. It wasn't the same since Glacies lost his powers.

Stone sipped some more beer and got another bitter taste when he thought of Glacies. Damned Glacies. He'd always had him down as weaker than he liked to pretend. And sure, he'd stepped up when the time was right. Helped bring down Saint.

But he always had this mopey attitude about him that made Stone's blood boil.

You're a superhero, alright? Get the hell over it. Suck that bottom lip in and do what you're supposed to do.

Then again, Stone was hardly one to talk, sitting here on his zillionth beer, just waiting until he'd had enough to black out again.

Vortex said his liver must be made of stone, too. Stone liked to test that out on a nightly basis. It usually ended in defeat, but not until he was absolutely—

The door rattled open. Stone found that strange, especially in a storm like this. Stone ignored it though, but he became more curious when he heard amazed whispers in a language he didn't recognize from the rest of the old fools sitting in the bar.

He turned around, and he almost fell off his stool.

There were three people standing opposite. Three people stepping into his present like ghosts from the past.

When he saw them, he tensed his fists and felt rock spread across his palms.

Cassie.

Glacies.

And... Glacies' idiot friend.

"Well, well. The old team."

Stone saw the shock on Glacies' face right away.

"What's that look? Pity?"

"Stone, we need to—"

"Don't say we need to talk. 'Cause there ain't nothing to talk about. Haven't you heard? There's a storm. A goddamn huge storm that's gonna wash you the hell away. Might wanna hide, seeing as you've got no powers anymore."

Glacies looked at his sister, then at his idiot pal, Damon, or something.

And then he turned back to Stone and tensed his fists.

When the ice spread across his palms, Stone couldn't exactly say he was surprised. Glacies always was a sneaky little shit. So either he'd rediscovered his abilities, or he'd just been keeping his abilities under wraps all along.

"Wow," Stone said, staggering closer to Glacies and his crew. "That what you've come to talk about? All this way to tell me you're a little liar?"

"I'm sorry for not being straight," Glacies said. "I... I understand me not being straight led to the—"

"To the Resistance falling apart, yeah. Yeah, you'd better be sorry for that. But you'd also better leave before I get too mad. You wouldn't like me when I'm mad."

"You're Stone," Glacies said. "Not the Hulk."

"Huh?"

"Nothing. Just... Stone, we need your help."

Stone widened his wandering eyes and started laughing. He laughed right from his belly as he looked from Cassie to Glacies to Damon and back to Glacies again. "You need my help, do you? You need my help now? Well where were you when I needed your help? Where have you been all this time when other people needed your help?"

"Stone, trust me," Cassie said. "We've talked about this—"

"You don't get to stop the conversation here. And you don't get to start it, either. You stopped mattering the second you decided you didn't want to be a part of the Resistance anymore."

"I screwed up," Glacies said. "But I'm here to put that right."

Stone stepped right up to Glacies. Right up, so he was inches from his face. "Well, good for you. I'm glad you've decided to get your shit in order. But it's a no from me, I'm afraid."

"Stone, please."

"I'm not here to satisfy your guilty conscience. I get why

your sister and your pal are going along with this, but I'm neither, so I won't. No more games."

"This isn't a game," Cassie said.

"So I suggest you walk before—"

"The people we're after could destroy every single ULTRA in existence, Stone."

Stone held his mouth open at that point. It was strange, because he certainly hadn't been all that bothered about self-destruction these last few months.

But that didn't exactly mean he couldn't care about other people. Other ULTRAs.

"The guy we're chasing. An ULTRA called Catalyst. He has something called the Failsafe. And if he finds a way to activate that Failsafe, every single ULTRA you've ever known falls."

Stone was still struggling to speak. He felt like he was losing ground in this argument, sobering up way more rapidly than he'd have liked—to a nasty headache. "And why should I give a shit?"

"Because if there's a part of you that's ever felt anything for any ULTRA, then you need to understand that all of that goes away if we don't stop Catalyst. If we don't get the Failsafe back. And it needs to be all of us, if we're to do this. All of us."

Stone glanced to Cassie. "He telling the truth?"

"Trust me," Cassie said, between biting her nails. "I think my brother's full of shit sometimes. But no word of a lie here. We need you, Stone."

Stone looked then at Damon.

"Yeah," Damon said, scratching his forearms. "Kyle isn't kidd—"

"Honestly don't give a shit about your opinion, chubs."

"Right," Damon said, nodding, his cheeks a shade of red. "Sure. I'll just, um. Yeah. I'll just stand over here and be quiet."

The four of them stood there in silence for a while, not saying a word. And the longer this silence went on, the more Stone thought about the people he'd cared about. The ULTRAs he'd cared about. The ones he still did care about. And how he didn't want to risk losing them at all.

"I can help."

A smile spread across Glacies' face. "Great. Then we—"

"But only if we have all of us together. All the old team."

Glacies' temporary elation wavered. "Stone, I... I don't know how to tell you this. But Ember. He's..."

Glacies didn't have to finish. Stone raised his hand. A silence filled the bar. A silence in memory of another lost soldier. "God bless him," Stone said.

He took a sip of a bottle that was sitting on a table beside him then he turned around, looking surprisingly more sober.

"I know where to find another troop," Stone said. He held out a rocky hand. "Teleport us back to my place."

"Your place? Where's—"

"Three blocks down."

Glacies nodded, then reluctantly reached for Stone's hand. Stone could see he was uncomfortable, which he had to admit amused him a little.

They held hands, the four of them. And although there was the addition of Damon, it was like a flashback to old times. To better times. Times of togetherness. Times of unity.

"On my count," Stone said. "Three—"

"I don't have to count."

"Well I do. I need to barf. And I'd rather barf in teleportation-land, if you don't mind. Three, two, one..."

I TELEPORTED the four of us over to Stone's place, being sure to check I wasn't covered in Stone-vom the second we landed.

I was soon distracted when I saw who was perched on the end of Stone's bed.

"What..." I said.

"Oh yeah," Stone said, rubbing the back of his head. "Yeah, we kinda hooked up. Sorry to beat you to her, brother. I know how much of a crush you used to have on her."

Stone patted me on the shoulder, and for the first time since we'd reunited, I saw that genuine mischievous smile on his face again.

Because on the edge of his bed, an old friend sat.

An old crush? Possibly.

Whatever.

It didn't matter either way.

It was Vortex.

30

"**W**ell. This is slightly awkward."

A sly grin tugged at Vortex's cheeks. "Only awkward if you make it awkward. How've you been?"

It seemed surreal, being reunited with Vortex all over again. To the point that I felt like I'd been blushing permanently ever since I found her sitting on the edge of Stone's bed. I'd always prepared myself for reunion with Vortex, and with the others. But there was something different about seeing Vortex again. Not to say she was my favorite, but... Well, yeah, I suppose she was my favorite.

As much as I loved Ellicia, there was always something about Vortex. Right from the day we'd first met. Not a crush, exactly. Just a kind of appreciation. Of understanding. Like we got each other in a way that the others didn't.

"I've been good," I said.

"Keeping out of trouble?"

"Something like that."

"I figured. Nothing on the news about you so realized you really had opted out for good. Thought it was a temporary fad, to be honest. Which, well... I guess it is. Seeing as you're here now."

I shrugged and wiped my forehead. I glanced out of the bedroom, toward the lounge, where Stone was catching up with Cassie, and Damon was standing there like a piece of wet lettuce. "How did you—"

"Stone and me? I guess it just kind of happened. We hung out a few times. He's a nice person. Things just went from there, really. You and that girl still together?"

"Ellicia? We... I guess. I dunno. Sort of."

"So no, in other words."

"It's complicated."

"It always is. Anyway. I appreciate you bringing Stone back here before he's completely inebriated. You must've said something really poignant to him to drag him out of that stupor."

"The drinking a problem?"

"Liver of stone, he says. Still waiting for proof of that."

"Huh."

"But something tells me you're not just here to escort Stone back home."

I sighed as the reality of the situation dawned once again. The urgency of what had to be done. Of the stakes involved.

I told Vortex about the Failsafe. About what it meant if we didn't get it out of the wrong hands. Of the risks and threats it posed to everyone. The old team. The new ULTRAs. Everyone.

She mulled my words over for a while. Sat there, staring intensely at her palms. I wondered whether to break the silence. In the other room, Stone, Cassie, and Damon hardly seemed to be getting on like a house on fire.

But it was Vortex who eventually broke the silence. "What we've got here. What we've worked to achieve. Some... some sense of normality. It's taken a lot, you know?"

I totally sympathized with Vortex. "I felt the same. That's

why I gave up who I really was. I didn't want to face this problem head on. But I've seen what I have to do now. Even if I only embrace Glacies one final time, I have to do it."

"It's not just the mental effects, Kyle. It's the physical effects."

I narrowed my eyes. "The physical effects? What physical effects?"

"You haven't had them either, then?"

I started to shake my head. Then Vortex rolled up her sleeves.

When I saw her arms, I felt sick.

"How did..."

"The bruises came first. Then they opened up and started weeping. I thought it was some kind of bite at first... or infection. But it turned out it only got worse whenever I used my abilities. Then there were the nosebleeds. And the unconsciousness. Using our powers. It might seem good right now. But it's not going to be good forever."

I swallowed a lump in my throat and tried to think of any time I'd had strange experiences. "This... might not happen to all of us. Respectfully."

Vortex pulled her sleeves back down. "Maybe. Maybe not. But it's happening to me. And I'm not sure how much further I can push."

I nodded. I understood Vortex's concerns. What she was getting at. But I had to make my point clear. "I understand. Totally. And I'm in no position to suggest this is a viable sacrifice for you to make. But if there's anything worth our sacrifice, it's surely the safety of not just the ULTRAs threatened by the Failsafe, but the chaos that could cause amongst everyone when that order finally topples again."

Vortex sighed. "I get it. I do. I just... Kyle, I don't know if I'm strong enough and I don't know if Stone's thinking straight. That's the truth. The honest truth."

"Stone says he's in."

"Stone says a lot of things. Look. I appreciate your concerns, but this isn't our fight. Not anymore."

"Then whose fight is it? Mine? Alone?"

"You're the strongest ULTRA. You were asked to do this task for a reason. I'm sorry. Really. But this isn't the old times anymore. Things have changed. Moved on. I really wish I could—"

Vortex didn't finish what she was saying.

Well, she might've. But I didn't hear it.

An explosion blasted through the road outside.

All of us rushed over to the door.

When we looked outside, my stomach dropped.

Catalyst was here.

And he was heading toward Stone's home.

31

I saw Catalyst standing on the road outside and I felt my stomach turn.

It was late afternoon. The rain was pouring now. The rest of this street looked totally empty, like life had been paused for Catalyst's arrival. I heard his heavy footsteps moving closer to us as the damp earth filled my nostrils. I couldn't taste anything but fear. Fear because he seemed capable of tracking me down no matter what. Fear because it didn't matter how far I got away from him, how long I was traveling, he always caught me up, like he was tracing me somehow.

"This the guy you're on about?" Stone grunted.

I nodded. "That's the guy."

Stone tensed his fists, which covered in rock.

Then he started to walk out of his house.

"Then you'd better let me formally introduce myself."

"Wait," I said.

I wasn't sure what it was that stopped me in my tracks. A combination of things, really. Sure, that curiosity as to how he'd found me after all this time. But also *why* he'd found me.

Catalyst had the Failsafe. He'd taken it from me.

So why had he come back for me?

"What the hell's keeping you?"

I looked at Stone. Then at Vortex, Damon, Cassie.

I felt responsible for them, all of a sudden. Like I was dragging them headfirst into my fight.

"We're with you," Vortex said. "Whether you like it or not."

I half-smiled at her, then turned back to face Catalyst.

I squeezed my palms and felt ice cover them.

"You made a mistake coming here," I said.

I walked into the rain, leading the way toward Catalyst. He was standing still now, the rain lashing down and bouncing off his black cloak. I still hadn't seen this guy's face. He was keeping it covered up, for whatever reason.

"You going to take that hood off and look me in the eye?" I said. "Or are you gonna just hide behind it forever?"

Catalyst tilted his head. He didn't say anything in response.

"Well?" I said. "What the hell are you here for?"

I saw a glimmer of Catalyst's smile then, just peeking from under his hood. I saw the pale skin. The scars.

And then he opened his mouth.

"To keep a promise I made. To finish you. Kyle Peters."

Before I could react, a massive blast of energy surged under my feet and sent me flying up into the sky. I was moving so fast that the rain felt like little daggers biting at my skin. I spun around, trying to re-balance myself, but then something punched into my right side and I went hurtling out of control again.

I closed my eyes and steadied myself. I was tougher than this clown and his telekinetic tricks. I might not be as tough as I once was, but I wasn't going to just back down.

I opened my eyes and held myself firm in the middle of the sky.

Catalyst was just inches away from me.

He lifted his hands and went to fire another burst of energy at me. But this time, I lifted my hands and blocked that energy before it could fly at me. I didn't know where my friends were. They couldn't be far below. But part of me didn't even want them to get involved in this, anyway. This was my fight. And I was going to win it.

"You can keep on trying to fight," I said. "But you won't win."

"You're so full of talk. That's your problem. You never, ever shut up."

"Wish I could say the same about you."

I shot two blasts of ice at Catalyst's face.

Then he just knocked them away like they were nothing but flies.

"You're making a mistake by resisting," Catalyst said. "You have no idea just how special you—"

Catalyst grabbed the sides of his head. He started shouting, crying out.

When I saw Vortex underneath him, I knew exactly why.

She was making him dream. And Vortex-induced dreams were never a nice thing.

I flew at him and knocked him back toward the ground. I was going to fly him so hard into the earth that it was going to kill him. Break all his bones and end him, once and for all.

"Where's the Failsafe?" I shouted.

Catalyst didn't respond.

I tightened my grip on him, flew even faster down.

"I asked you a question. Where's the—"

I felt a hard punch to my kidneys. So hard that it pounded the power right out of me.

And then he pressed an anti-energy gun against my stomach, fired, and shot Vortex out of the sky.

And all of a sudden he was on top of me.

He was the one flying the pair of us down.
Pushing me down, right toward the earth.
I tried to struggle. I tried to kick back. I tried to fight.
But it was no good.
We were crashing to the surface of the earth.
And there wasn't a thing I could do about it.

32

I felt myself surging to the earth below and I knew my time was numbered.

I looked past Catalyst at the bright sky above. It looked so peaceful, so serene. And in a way, as the pair of us moved in what felt like slow motion now, I felt totally calm. I'd lost. Simple as that. I'd lost and everything was over.

I had no more responsibilities to worry about. I had no more fight to give.

And I had nobody expecting a thing of me. Not anymore.

Finally, I was heading back to normality.

It was just a shame that normality meant I probably wasn't going to be around to witness it.

I heard shouting. In the corner of my eyes, I saw my friends and my family emerging. Damon. Stone. Cassie. Vortex. They looked at me with shock as they tried to fly toward Catalyst. But they couldn't get close. They just bounced off an invisible barrier before they could get anywhere near.

I looked up at Catalyst's face and I saw him, then. For the first real time, I saw him underneath that hood. I saw the pale skin. The scars covering his cheeks.

And I saw the gaps where his eyes once were.

And as I saw him, it clicked. He was blind. That's why he hadn't recognized me right away. He couldn't see me.

But hell. He might be blind. But his other senses sure as hell made up for that.

I looked over my shoulder and in this weird, slowed-down time, I realized I was just inches away. My powers, Catalyst was repressing them with that anti-energy gun he had pushed into my belly.

And I knew I could fight. If I really wanted to, I could fight.

But I wasn't strong enough anymore.

All my fight had gone.

I prepared to slam into the ground.

And then the image of everyone that was going to fall—everyone I cared about—because of me giving up filled my mind and made me grit my teeth.

I couldn't give in.

I couldn't afford to.

I...

I realized then I'd stopped. Both of us had stopped. We were hovering right above the ground.

I didn't understand it. Not at first.

Then I saw that Catalyst was bleeding.

He was bleeding, and that blood was dripping down onto me.

I didn't know where the blood had come from. But wherever it came from, it distracted Catalyst enough to loosen his grip on me, making my fall to the ground much less painful than it could've been.

I rolled over to the right, still not sure of what was happening, not quite understanding what I was witnessing.

And then it clicked.

It clicked. Hard.

I didn't totally understand still. I wasn't sure how it was possible. How this was happening.

But slowly, I started to see movement.

Really fast movement.

There was someone attacking Catalyst.

Someone really quick.

"A hand here would be nice!"

Right away, I flew at Catalyst. As too did Stone, Vortex, Cassie and Damon.

The five of us hurtled toward him. He was totally cornered now. And we were strong. Together, we were strong.

Catalyst looked around at us as we all surrounded him, that speedy attacker still flying at him, disorienting him, sending him out of control.

Then when we were inches away and I was about to fire a blast of ice at him, Catalyst turned and looked right at me.

"You'll never take the Failsafe from me."

"Want a bet?"

He smiled, blood dribbling down his chin. "There are things you still don't understand. Goodbye, Glacies."

I shot the ice at him.

Cassie and Damon fired purple electricity at him.

Stone pulled his fists back and went to crack them either side of his head.

Vortex's eyes rolled back and prepared to send him into a bout of nightmares.

But before we could attack, Catalyst had gone.

We all stopped ourselves before we could attack. With the exception of Damon, who accidentally sent four blasts of electricity into the sky, much to the derision of Stone.

"This guy's a new troop of ours?" he grunted.

Damon blushed. "Sorry. I... I guess I just..."

Whatever Damon said next, I didn't process. Not really.

Because there was somebody opposite me who I hadn't seen for a long time.

Someone I thought we'd lost. A casualty of the Resistance.

At the very least, I was convinced their powers were gone.

But not on that evidence. Not on that evidence at all.

She slowed down and finally came into view. When she did, she smiled at me. "Surprise," she said.

"Roadrunner," I said, unable to keep the smile from my face.

33

"So what now?"

They weren't the three words I was hoping for, really. Because whenever anyone asked "what now?" usually it was directed at me, especially if it was ULTRA related.

A few days ago, I would've recoiled at being asked what the plan was. I would've shaken my head, done everything I could to avoid making a decision.

But circumstances had changed. The stakes had changed.

Catalyst had got away again. He still had the Failsafe.

And stronger than my will to no longer be a hero—to give up my Glacies status—was the urge to get that Failsafe back and take Catalyst down. Even if that meant the whole world finding out I had abilities once more.

"Glacies?" Stone asked. "You just gonna stand there looking like a tool or you actually gonna pitch in here?"

I looked around at Stone. By his side, Vortex. Cassie. Damon. And now Roadrunner. I smiled when I saw Roadrunner. I still couldn't believe she was back. And sure, there was a bit of guilt there about the way things had gone when we'd last fought alongside each other. But mostly it seemed like water under the bridge.

She hadn't said a lot. She'd appeared out of nowhere. So I had to assume all was good, anyway.

She hadn't tried to kill me. Yet. That had to count for something.

"Where'd he come from?" Vortex asked. "How... how'd he find us?"

"I can answer that," Roadrunner said, stepping forward and breaking her silence.

In her hands, she held some kind of device. A tablet device.

"I found this tucked in his pants."

Stone's eyes widened. "You went down his pants?"

"All in the name of saving the world, I guess."

She put it in my hands.

It was a tablet-style computer. And on that tablet, in the middle of the screen, a blinking red dot. Surrounding that blinking red dot, a Google Maps style overlay.

And when I zoomed out, it didn't take a genius for me to figure out that this was a map pointing out where I was.

I was the red dot.

"How did—ow!"

I felt pain in the back of my neck. A real searing pain, like something had stung me.

But then when I saw Roadrunner's bloodied hand holding on to something, I realized I hadn't been stung at all.

"Looks like you had some kind of tracking device put inside you," Roadrunner said. "A way of him figuring out where you're at."

I frowned. "But... but he's never had long enough to do that to me."

"Then maybe someone else did it to you. I dunno. You're the genius. Figure it out."

I frowned as I looked at the little metal chip Roadrunner had dropped into my palm. That thing had been in my neck all this time? When had Catalyst done that to me? When could he possibly have...

It clicked, then.

Maybe Catalyst didn't do it to me at all.

Maybe Michael Williamson did it to me to keep an eye on where I was at. I didn't exactly give him my approval, but it'd make sense.

The bad news?

If my suspicions were right, then that meant something bad had happened to Michael Williamson. Something terrible, for him to have to give up his tracking device.

But even so. Why was Catalyst so determined to find me when he had the Failsafe?

What more did he want?

"So I asked a while ago but nobody's answered me," Stone said, gritting his teeth quite audibly. "What the hell's the plan?"

I wanted to answer Stone. But I was still too curious about Roadrunner's return to think about anything else.

"While you were away," I said, walking right up to Roadrunner. "Your powers. How did you..."

She turned around and looked at me, narrowing her eyes. She opened her mouth, getting ready to talk. Then she smiled, shook her head. "That's another story for another time. Another comic for another superhero. Huh?"

I wasn't totally satisfied with the answer. But for now, I knew it'd have to do.

"What matters now is I don't have long here to help you with what's going on. I have my own battles to fight. My own things to think about. My own responsibilities. But I caught wind you needed help and hey, here I am. Looks like I was in the right place at the right time."

"And we appreciate it," I said. "Seriously."

Roadrunner nodded. There was still a glassiness to her eyes though that hinted to me that she was still holding something back. "Anyway. Stone's got a point. What is your plan? And don't tell me you've done something stupid like given up making plans for everyone, too."

I saw everyone looking at me, waiting for their answer.

Then behind us, I heard footsteps. Voices. I looked over my shoulder and saw people walking toward us. Locals, a whole crowd of them. They'd come out of their homes, out of hiding. They'd clearly witnessed what had happened with Catalyst.

A balding man with a thick white beard, missing a few teeth at the front, came up to me and glared at me with wide, bulging eyes. "Glacies?" he asked. "Glacies?"

I felt my stomach tense, my arms shake, and I felt myself turning in all over again, like a snail hiding inside its shell for protection.

"Glacies?" more people muttered, surrounding me. "Glacies?"

I looked over at Cassie and I saw her lowering her head. Daring me to step up. To accept who I was, finally. To stop running away from my problems and my responsibilities and to face them, head on.

"Glacies?"

Then I turned to the crowd and smiled.

I took a deep breath.

Tensed my fists.

Ice spread up my arms, and I hovered just above them.

"Glacies," I said, nodding. "Glacies."

I saw the momentary shock and panic on their faces and for a moment I was convinced they were going to start attacking me.

Instead, they fell to their knees and started cheering. Applauding. Crying, even.

As I looked around at the people of this small Indonesian village then, I knew how much I was needed. How much my order, my status, was respected.

I knew that I might be ready to finish being Glacies.

But the world wasn't ready for Glacies to go away just yet.

And it was time to honor that.

34

Catalyst sat alone with the Failsafe, gradually feeling weaker.

It was dark where he was, in the middle of the Mojave Desert. It was cool at night. So cool. Hard to believe a place so warm in the day could be so cool at night. But he liked the solitude. He liked being away from everyone else. He liked being at one with the darkness that he was cast under by his lack of vision, anyway.

Besides, he needed time to recharge.

It started with the showdown with Glacies. He'd been so close to ramming him into the ground. So close to finishing him off. Or at least creating the *illusion* that he'd finished him off. Because Catalyst had no intentions of finishing Glacies off at all. Glacies was important.

But if he could just make everyone else *think* that Glacies was finished, well, it'd be easier for the world to understand. It'd be easier to succeed at his goals without much of a fight.

His ears were ringing. He could taste vomit and blood creeping up his throat. Every inch of his body shook, like he had a nasty fever. He wasn't sure how long he'd felt this ill. He couldn't pinpoint it, not exactly.

Only that he'd started feeling weaker every time he used his abilities.

That came to a head when he'd been attacked when he was so close to making Glacies disappear with him just hours ago.

He'd been so close. Then some ULTRA he didn't know about attacked him, disoriented him. And usually he'd be fine just swatting another ULTRA away, like the pest they were. Usually, he'd have the composure and the strength to deal with them.

But not this time.

This time, he'd been unable to recompose himself. He'd kept on getting attacked by that ULTRA, who could move extremely fast, and in the end it had distracted him, disoriented him.

He'd floated there, the remains of the Resistance flying at him, and he'd had a choice. Keep on fighting, or retreat.

And he'd chosen retreat.

As much as he needed Glacies, he'd chosen to retreat.

He leaned back, his neck stiff. He could feel the smooth metal of the Failsafe in his hand. He knew his tracking device was gone. That'd make locating Glacies much more difficult.

But it wasn't going to stop him.

It wasn't going to get in his way.

It couldn't. Because if he let it get in his way, then everything he'd spent so many years working toward was over.

He looked up at the sky and sensed its blackness, its emptiness. And yet it wasn't empty. Not at all. There were so many stars up there. And around those stars, there were so many more planets. An uncountable number.

And that was only in this universe.

He didn't even want to think about the other universes that

must be out there. The universes that existed in some kind of parallel reality to his own.

He just knew he could feel something getting closer.

Something accelerating rapidly toward this universe, toward this galaxy, toward this planet.

And whatever it was, it was making him feel sicker.

Which is why he had to activate the Failsafe before he didn't have the strength left to do so.

He stood up, stumbling to his feet. He took a few steadying breaths of the cool desert air. Total silence all around him. Well. It would've been to someone else. But Catalyst could hear every flutter of a bird's wing miles away. He could hear the footstep of an insect; smell the aviation fuel of an airplane passing overhead.

He steadied his breathing and then he looked back up at the sky, feeling that gravitational pull dragging something closer. Something he didn't totally understand. Something he wasn't even sure he'd be alive to face, head on.

Then he looked down at the Failsafe, caressed it between his fingers.

He'd find Glacies because of what he'd learned from Michael Williamson when he put him through unimaginable pain.

The Failsafe was not complete without the Source.

The pair of them went together, like a key in a lock.

And he knew exactly where to get to the Source. How to get to the Source.

But he had to find a new tactic, now he'd lost his tracking device. He had to find a way to draw that source toward him. Like squeezing puss from a zit.

And he had an idea.

He had a very good idea.

He bent his knees and jumped up into the sky, leaving a shockwave of dust beneath.

He'd draw Glacies toward him.

And this time, when he'd lured him close, he'd be ready.

There was no room for failure.

Not anymore.

35

Of all the tasks I had to do before fully committing myself to taking down Catalyst and retrieving the Failsafe, you wouldn't believe what I found one of the most difficult tasks in my life so far.

San Francisco looked good in fall. Orange leaves coated the hilly streets. I could hear the sounds of horns honking gently, not with the same ferocity and impatience as they did back in New York. The Golden Gate Bridge always looked spectacular as it soared over the Golden Gate Strait. Granted, there had been a little repair work needed after the showdown with Saint. There were few places in the world that hadn't been touched by that battle in some way.

But it didn't matter. San Francisco still looked stunning. It was rebuilding. Getting itself back to full strength, as was everywhere else.

I hovered to the right, past a few more ULTRAs I saw playing in the street. It was strange seeing ULTRAs just going about their lives and people accepting them. For so long, being an ULTRA had been such a secret thing. A thing to be paranoid about. But now it was much more normal. More mainstream, after Adam re-distributed powers.

The irony being that the most famous ULTRA of all—yours truly—was still keeping his identity under wraps for the most part.

Until now.

I floated down by the apartments right near San Francisco University. I'd found out where Ellicia was living now. She hadn't moved in long ago, but she'd left her details and told me to get in touch when I was ready.

Well I was ready now. I was here and I was ready.

But I wasn't going to tell her what she wanted to hear. Not exactly.

I was going to tell her the truth. The whole truth. About who I was. Who I *still* was.

And what I had to do.

I landed by the entrance to her apartment block and pulled my hood up. As much as I accepted who I was going to be—Glacies—this visit was personal, and I didn't want to get hounded right now. I walked up to it, and realized there was a student ID required. I scratched the back of my neck. Typical. I wanted to come here, and I wanted things to go as smoothly as possible, and already obstacles were mounting up in my way.

I saw a girl walking between the apartments.

"Scuse me?" I called.

She looked around and smiled.

I pointed at the card reader. "Lost my keycard. Can't get in. You mind giving me a hand?"

She walked up to the glass, smiling.

Then she shook her head.

"It's girls only in here," she said. "Nice try, creep."

She turned and walked away, leaving me a little embarrassed.

I sighed, trying to battle my blushing cheeks. I'd have to use my abilities to get inside. But that'd just make me look even more of a creep if this girl saw me again. I had to watch my step.

I held my breath and walked right through the glass.

Then I made myself disappear and crept up the stairs toward Ellicia's apartment. Apartment 8.

When I was outside, I saw the girl who'd called me a creep at the door walking inside. I sneaked in, quickly, remaining invisible. So this girl lived with Ellicia. Interesting. Oh well. It was weird she hadn't recognized me. It was rare for me to not be recognized these days. I kind of liked that she hadn't, though. But at the same time, I was kind of pissed that if I *hadn't* been recognized, I'd just be regarded as a creep. Yeah, that wasn't so good at all.

I headed down the corridor and looked in each and every room, feeling particularly creepy at seeing girls inside each of them. I started to get nervous that maybe I'd ended up in the wrong apartment when I turned and saw the dark-haired girl who'd stopped me at the door standing right opposite me, and looking right at me.

"Nice try with the invisibility, Glacies," she said. "I can see right through you."

"If you could see right through me then—then that'd mean the invisibility's working."

She paused, clearly taken aback by my nervous outburst. "Well. Not technically. The opposite to that. Whatever. Doesn't have the same ring to it. But anyway. I suggest you get the hell outta here."

I debated keeping my invisibility active just in case she was calling my bluff in some way.

But in the end, I dropped it and realized right then that someone in America now knew I had my powers for sure.

"Didn't think you had your powers anymore," the girl said, smiling smugly. "Anything else you've lied to Ellicia about?"

"Look," I said, my cheeks blushing again. "I just want to see her."

"Well, you had your chance to see her. That chance has gone now. So I suggest you turn around and—"

"Kyle?"

I heard her voice and immediately felt every inch of stress in my body melting away.

I turned and saw her standing by the kitchen area. She looked into my eyes and I looked into hers, and it felt like we were meeting for the first time all over again. Connecting like we'd never connected before. Like it was all so fresh but all so familiar at the same time.

"It's okay, Ellicia," the girl said. "I've told him to leave."

"Ellicia, I'm sorry," I said.

"Don't listen to—"

"Kerry, just give us a second. Okay?"

The girl—Kerry—looked taken aback by Ellicia's frankness. She shook her head and walked away. "Your funeral."

We both waited until Kerry's footsteps had disappeared before we started talking.

"Ellicia, I—"

"Kyle, I didn't mean to—"

"There's something I need to tell you."

"You still have your abilities?"

"I still have my... wait. How did you—"

"It was obvious, Kyle."

"Really?"

"Well, maybe not to everyone. But I know you. I know when you're acting differently. I know when you're hiding things."

I lowered my head and looked at the floor. "I guess you do. But why didn't you confront me if you knew?"

Ellicia's eyes broke contact with mine. "Because... because I wanted to believe you were doing the right thing, too. I wanted things to work out for you. I wanted you to find some kind of normality, even if it meant living a lie."

I swallowed a lump in my throat. "I'm sorry you felt you had to keep it a secret from me."

"Well, it's out now. And here we are. Both on different paths, but together. Right?"

She smiled at me, and I smiled back. And for a moment, I thought about just joining Ellicia in this life. Turning my back on the Resistance, on pursuing Catalyst, on seeking out the Failsafe.

But I knew that wasn't an option. It was just pulling the wool over my eyes a little longer.

"There's something I have to do," I said, walking up to Ellicia and taking her hands in mine. "Somewhere... somewhere dangerous I have to go. And this time I... I'm not sure I'll make it out alive."

Ellicia leaned in and kissed my lips and in that moment I really believed this moment would last forever.

Then she pulled away, rested her forehead on mine, looked up into my eyes. "You will come back. Because you always do. And when you do, the world will be a better place again."

I stood in the corridor with Ellicia, holding her, resting my head against hers, for what felt like forever.

"Now go on," she said, backing away. "There's people waiting for you."

She walked back to one of the other rooms inside the apartment. And I couldn't help feeling proud of her. So proud. She'd done so well to make it this far. She'd succeeded so much to make it to college. "You're going to do amazing here," I said.

"I'll need your help," she said, flickering a smile my way. "Especially if I'm gonna get top grades."

I smiled back. But this time I had to wipe my eyes. Because it felt like we were pretending. When in all truth, both of us knew things were never going to be the same again, if I ever did make it out of my battle with Catalyst, which I was doubting more by the second.

"Go do what you have to do," Ellicia said.

"And you too."

I watched her walk into her friend's room.

"I love y..."

I didn't get to finish what I was saying.

Ellicia was already gone.

I teleported myself back outside her apartment and drifted into the air, high above, hovering right over San Francisco Bay.

I looked across the bay at the warm, bright sun and I thought of Ellicia.

"You going to be moping here all day, or..."

I jumped, almost falling out of the sky.

When I turned my head, I saw Roadrunner looking right at me, smile on her face.

"When did..."

"Doesn't matter when. What matters is why."

She handed me a phone, which had a map on it, and a red dot.

"What is this?"

"Let's just say I've picked up a few new tricks in my time away. And let's just say I've gone on a little journey while you've been saying bye-bye to your girl."

I frowned at the phone, at the map. "I still don't get what I'm looking at."

She pointed at the dot and tapped on it with a long, painted fingernail. "This, my friend, is Catalyst's location."

I looked into her eyes, adrenaline coursing through my bloodstream. "How do you..."

"Again, that's irrelevant. But we're going to have to act fast if we want to get to him. This place is the Source. It's where he activates the Failsafe and, well. Relieves us of our duties. He won't stick around forever. So are you ready?"

I looked down at SFU. At Ellicia's apartment. I imagined the life she'd be going ahead to live. The fun she'd be having.

But all that seemed so alien to me.

Because it was.

I clutched my fists and felt ice cover my body.

I looked at Roadrunner, and I nodded.

"Ready," I said.

"Good," she said, smiling. "Then let's go finish this."

36

"Seriously, man. What is it with you and volcanoes?"

The Resistance and I flew toward Mount Vesuvius in Italy. It was night, and a cold night at that. Specks of rain lashed down on us the closer we got to this volcano, which Roadrunner had tracked Catalyst too using... well. I wasn't totally sure what she was using. Just that she was certain that volcano was where he'd headed, and also she'd seemed to have changed quite a lot since we'd last met. I expected her to be furious about how things had gone down. How I'd been forced to leave her in Adam's company, totally weak and powerless.

But she was back, and she was different. And for all her secrets, she seemed determined to help.

I saw the mountains approaching in the distance and I felt sick to my gut. We were getting close to the volcano, no doubt about that. I wasn't sure why I was so nervous. I was still strong. I was still Glacies, after all. I had no reason to worry or panic. I was strong, even if I'd tried to convince myself otherwise for so long now.

But something was niggling at me. Something was telling

me that this was a bad decision. That there was just something so... off about all this.

Still, I didn't have any choice but to progress. And it seemed like Stone, Vortex, Roadrunner, Cassie and Damon were all sticking by my side too.

Because Vesuvius had to be the Source.

The Source where the Failsafe could be activated.

"You know, I could kinda get used to this whole hero thing."

I turned to Damon, slightly bemused. "Say that again when you've been involved in a massive battle."

Damon grinned. "Oh I will. I mean, it's gotta beat normal life, right? Reality and all that. Boring reality."

"You shouldn't take normality for granted."

"Hell, I just love this. I love that I'm stronger than I thought I was. I love that I can do things I never imagined I'd be able to in my wildest dreams." He shot a burst of electricity into the sky, the beaming grin on his face as he got to grips with flying infectious.

"Yeah, well," I said. "You just be careful. Watch yourself. Y'know?"

"Oh, I will. I'll..."

I saw the flash of light in the corner of my eye in slow motion.

A burst of energy coming toward us.

No, wait.

Not just a burst of energy.

A pile of rocks.

"Watch out!"

I charged in front of the Resistance and froze the rocks in midair. Wherever they were coming from, I knew for a fact that someone had thrown them at us. And process of elimination made it pretty obvious who exactly had thrown them.

Some of the rocks slipped through. I watched Stone smash

them with his fists, Roadrunner zooming around and swatting the smaller pieces of debris away so they didn't pierce anyone's skin.

Best of all, I saw my best friend and my sister side by side, firing the smaller pieces of rock away.

"On your right, Glacies!"

I turned around and saw a huge mass of rock just inches from snapping my head from my neck.

I lifted my hands and I stopped it. I stopped it, right there in midair.

I used all my strength to hold it back, biting down on my bottom lip, tasting blood.

"Do you need a hand?"

I ignored Stone's voice.

I opened up a wormhole right behind the mass of rock.

And I sent it right into that wormhole.

I'd opened the other end of the wormhole up right inside the volcano where Catalyst was. Hopefully he enjoyed that gift.

The moment I threw the rock through the wormhole, I saw explosions to our left.

"Shit," Stone said. "Damn good job we didn't just go teleporting in there."

Stone had a point. I had a feeling Catalyst wouldn't just leave the Source open to teleportation. There'd be some kind of booby trap. Something rigged right at where I'd exit the wormhole.

"Looks like we're taking the good ol'fashioned way," Cassie said.

I faced the volcano where the explosions had just eased and so too did everyone else. "Looks like that's the case."

I surged toward the volcano. We couldn't mess around anymore. Sure, there might be other distractions. There might be other traps. But it was the choice between a little recklessness that might kill us, or a lack of recklessness that would definitely kill us.

I knew which option I wanted to take.

I hurtled toward the opening of the volcano. There couldn't be long left. If Catalyst was here at the Source, then that meant he wasn't afraid to activate the Failsafe, even if it killed him in the process.

I got closer to the mouth of the volcano, then I saw something rising up out of it.

"Is... is that what I think it is?" Damon asked.

"It depends what you think it is," Stone said. "But to me, it looks a hell of a lot like lava."

A mass of lava rose out of the top of the volcano. It moved toward us, slowly. I had no doubts about dealing with it if I had enough time. I just wasn't sure I had enough time.

"Um, Kyle?" Damon said. "You actually gonna do something here, or..."

I looked beyond the lava and I saw Catalyst standing down at the pit of the volcano, the Failsafe in his hand.

I knew he'd seen me too, even though he was miles away.

I sensed a smile flick across his face. I thought I heard him speak, as if it was from within me.

Then the next thing I knew, the lava was inches from my body.

I rose my hands into the air. Dragged a thick wall of ice out in front of myself, in front of the Resistance. It melted right upon contact with the lava. So I fired even thicker ice. Even thicker and thicker, trying to contain it all.

But it wasn't holding. It was still melting. I couldn't cover the entire lava wave.

"How comfortable are you guys with being icy?" I asked.

No response.

"Guys? How..."

When I looked back, something made my skin crawl.

The Resistance was gone.

Every single one of them.

I turned back to the lava wave and saw a huge gap in the middle of it, leading right down toward Catalyst.

"What the hell have you done with them?"

I covered myself in ice and threw myself through that lava hole. I felt myself getting hotter, burning up, but just kept on laying layer after layer of ice around myself, until eventually I was through the lava wave, and I was inside that volcano, Catalyst underneath me.

"I said, what the hell have you—"

Catalyst opened up the Failsafe. That bright light peeked out of its sides. "I'd be careful before making your next move. Wouldn't want to risk anything reckless. Anything that might put anyone you care about at risk."

I became aware then of shouting. And when I looked around, I saw that the Resistance—my friends, my family—were all dangling in midair. As was the mass of lava, right above the volcano.

"One wrong move, I let it drop. Everything."

"You wouldn't."

"Try me," Catalyst said. His hood was down completely. I could see his bald face, empty of eyes. I wanted to know what had happened to him. How he'd reached this state. Part of me pitied him.

But mostly I just wanted to kick his ass.

"This can end, right here. You can hand me the Failsafe and we can let it go. All of it."

Catalyst studied my face for a second. He couldn't see me, not visually. But I got the sense he was looking right at me in other ways.

"Catalyst. This can end. You don't have to kill all our kind just to prove whatever point you're trying to prove. Just... just let go."

Catalyst was silent for a few more seconds.

Then he started laughing.

His laughing gave me the creeps. Especially with the light coming from the Failsafe in his hand, the lava he was holding above, and my friends, trapped underneath it.

"What's so funny?"

"You don't understand, do you?" he asked. "You really don't understand."

"Don't understand what?"

He looked at the Failsafe. "What this really is."

I narrowed my eyes. "What..."

"Anyway. You mentioned 'letting go'."

He looked up and flicked his middle finger.

I heard a cry.

When I looked up, I saw Damon tumbling clumsily into the lava.

He had seconds to live.

37

Catalyst could activate that Failsafe in the space of a second, but it didn't matter.

Not when my best friend was flying at a wall of lava.

I raced toward him, teleporting through the air. I started to feel weaker, like this entire volcano was suffocating my abilities.

Damon was just inches from the lava.

I could see the orange glow bouncing off his face.

I raised my hands and let out a cry. It was the most forceful, pained cry ever to leave my body. I let out all my anger at Catalyst. All my anger at Saint, at Adam, at everyone who'd stood in my way before.

And when I let out that cry, I felt ice blasting from my entire body.

I knocked Damon out of the way of the lava wall and went flying inside the lava myself.

Initially, I felt sheer agony. Intense, suffocating heat, hotter than anything I'd ever felt.

But the very fact that I was still comprehending those sensations meant I was alive.

I was still here.

I looked around and saw I was covered in a thick skin of ice. The lava wasn't even slightly piercing through it. Sheer instinct had kicked in, keeping me alive.

I let out another cry and I felt the lava turn hard all around me.

Then I stretched my arms either side and smashed the frozen lava into tiny pieces.

When the lava disappeared, falling everywhere but onto Catalyst, I checked first that everyone was okay. Damon was alive. That was the main thing. As was Cassie. As was everyone.

They were still hovering above, though. Which meant Catalyst was still holding them there with telekinetic force.

Which was a good thing. Because I wanted to deal with Catalyst myself.

I landed right opposite him. He was still holding the Failsafe open, light beaming from it. Catalyst was smiling, like he wasn't too surprised that I'd survived.

"You made it," he said.

"Of course I made it. Now where were we?"

I went to throw myself at the Failsafe.

Then I had a flashback.

It was inexplicable. Something I couldn't really get my head around. But that light. That glowing white light that came from the Failsafe.

It felt familiar.

Like I'd... felt it before.

I stopped, and I saw Catalyst's smile grow wider.

"Do you see now?"

Suddenly, everything felt very alien. Like the pieces were falling into place all around me, even if I didn't totally understand them yet.

"You were easier to lure here than I imagined. But now

you're here, we can get on with what we're really here for. Can't we?"

I didn't have time to react as Catalyst threw a paralyzing bolt of electricity at my chest. It sent me tumbling to my knees, suffocating me and my powers right there.

Catalyst's heavy footsteps walked over to me. He stood over me, looking down at me, that arrogant grin still on his face.

"You thought you'd come to the Source, didn't you?" he asked. "You poor boy. You thought you'd come to the Source. When in fact, you *are* the source."

Everything clicked, then. The reason Catalyst had lured me here. Why he'd been determined to capture me even after he'd got the Failsafe. "How... How am I—"

"Michael Williamson," Catalyst said. "Our mutual friend. He told me where to find the Source. Well. He didn't *tell* me exactly. It took a lot to get the truth from him. But when I found out the Source wasn't a place but a *someone*, well. I shouldn't have been surprised that that someone was the most powerful ULTRA now, should I?"

My heart raced. I was the Source. I was the thing that activated the Failsafe. Inside me, the power to destroy every one of my kind.

"Then why would... why would Michael send me after the Failsafe? If he knew how dangerous it was when it was with me?"

Catalyst's smile spread as he walked around me in a circle. "I discovered a secret from Michael a long time ago. A secret that you'll be very interested to hear. See, at first, I thought the Failsafe would give me power over the ULTRAs around me. But when I discovered what it's really capable of... well. I saw then that it was much, much more dangerous than an ULTRA off-switch."

"I don't understand."

"The Failsafe isn't an ULTRA off-switch. It doesn't have the ability to destroy every ULTRA. Or any ULTRA, except you. It is, in fact, something else entirely."

He let that statement hang. Like he was just begging me to ask him what its purpose was.

"It's a weapon," Catalyst said.

I struggled against the paralyzing energy crippling my body. Above, I heard the shouts and cries of my peers. The night sky outside the volcano seemed to be getting darker and darker. "Well, duh."

"But it's not the kind of weapon you think it is. It's a failsafe *against* the Failsafe."

I narrowed my eyes, unable to wrap my head around what Catalyst was saying. "That doesn't make any sense."

"Michael Williamson was many things. But he loved his ULTRAs more than he loved people. He figured if the ULTRAs were ever threatened in any way, he could use a failsafe of his own. A failsafe with the ability to wipe out the entire human race."

He looked at the glowing metal ball in his hand, then turned back to me, smiling.

"A bomb. A bomb with enough power to wipe the planet of humans in an instant. The kind of power only the strongest ULTRAs have inside of them."

"No."

"And you are the key."

"That's not... He wouldn't do that. He wouldn't—"

"Michael used you, Kyle. He used you because he wanted you to be a part of the arms race that everyone in the know wanted to win. Including himself. And he wanted you because he needed you. To destroy humanity."

I shook my head, unable to accept what I was hearing.

Michael had used me so that he could have me and the Failsafe together in one place.

And once I'd got that Failsafe to him... he was going to use it to wipe out humanity?

"The group who ended up in possession of the Failsafe," Catalyst said. "The one in Australia. Who you kindly broke into and stole it from."

"No," I said, unable to accept I was culpable in this mess in any way.

"They were government. And they were just trying their best to bury this Failsafe. To destroy it somehow, forever, so its powers could never be utilized. And you went storming right on in there and started the greatest arms race in the history of ULTRAkind. Without even realizing what you were doing."

I kneeled there, shaking my head. I felt empty. All that time I'd resisted responsibility. I'd fought against the urge to become a hero again. I'd wanted to be normal.

And when I'd finally taken a call of duty, I'd been used.

All along, I'd been used.

"But anyway," Catalyst said. "I figured I'll show you a little example of this failsafe's powers. Just a sample."

He lifted my finger telekinetically and no matter how hard I resisted, he cut the tip of it.

A little of my blood dripped into the light. And when it hit that light, I saw the light turning red.

Then I felt something.

Something building inside my body.

Inside my heart.

"The beauty of this failsafe?" Catalyst said. "Because *you* are the source, it tends to hone in on those you care about first."

"No!" I shouted.

"So do your best to keep a clear mind, Glacies. I'd hate for anyone you care about to get..."

I didn't hear anything after that.

I just heard a blast of high-pitched static squeal through my skull.

I let out a cry, and I felt something leave my chest. Something sharp. Something piercing.

And I tried to keep a clear mind.

I really, really tried to.

But when that sharp pain jolted from my chest, when that burst of red energy ripped its way out of my body, I knew who it was heading to.

I knew exactly who it was heading to.

And it broke my heart.

38

Ellicia was enjoying college. She really was.
But a part of her longed for home.
For Kyle.

It was night, and Ellicia had opted against going out. She'd been out partying a few nights in a row now. She couldn't drink, not legally, but try telling a bunch of newcomers not to drink when they'd all moved out of home and into a new city.

But honestly, Ellicia hadn't been all that fussed about drinking. She hadn't been bothered about partying.

She had a headache. And it was getting worse.

And she knew exactly why she had that headache.

She lay back on her single bed and stared up at the ceiling. She could hear horns honking outside. Strange how different the sounds of a different city could be. In a sense, there was nothing really different. There were lots of cars buzzing past. The chatter of people. The clatter of cutlery in restaurants and glasses in bars. But it just felt so different to New York. So different to home.

Besides, she was missing Kyle.

She hadn't taken the decision to move away from New York

lightly. SFU offered an amazing course in marine biology, something she was passionate about, and always had been. But to be honest, before things started going sour with Kyle, she'd never even considered moving this far away from home.

She'd felt like she needed a clean break. And she saw now it's because she knew all along that Kyle wasn't being totally honest with her about his abilities.

She'd seen the look in his eyes when faced with situations he was supposed to resolve. She'd seen the guilt that engulfed him when he *wanted* to act but couldn't, because he was, after all, still just eighteen-year-old Kyle Peters underneath his Glacies persona.

And eighteen-year-old Kyle Peters was just as entitled to a life as the rest of the world.

Ellicia's headache started to grow more intense. Her taste buds were spent, so the thought of tasteless food or drink made her feel sick. She'd been told about first-week flu before. Only this didn't feel like flu. It felt more like homesickness.

She got out of bed and walked over to her window. She opened it and stood there for a while, just taking deep breaths of the cool night air, listening to the sirens in the distance, watching the planes descend overhead. Wherever Kyle was, whatever he'd gone to do, it seemed important.

She couldn't shake the dread she'd felt when they'd exchanged that final glance. When he'd said those final words.

Because to Ellicia, as much as she hated to admit it, it felt like Kyle was saying goodbye.

A knock at her door made her jump. She turned around, looked at it. She was sure everyone else in her apartment had gone out. So who could it be?

She crept toward the door, heart thumping. She didn't want to call out. If it was a roommate, she wanted them to think she was asleep or something.

Then the door banged again. Harder, this time.

Ellicia stopped. She stopped right by the door and waited.

There was silence. A silence that stretched on for a long, long time.

She swallowed a lump in her throat and—

A searing pain.

A searing pain split through her skull, like she'd been hit over the head with something heavy.

She felt crippling sickness in her gut, like a load of razor blades were swirling around in there.

The taste returned to her mouth, and all she could taste was blood.

But those weren't even the worst things.

The worst thing was the sound.

A screaming.

A human screaming.

"You okay in there?"

Ellicia snapped back into reality just as suddenly as she'd jolted out of it. She felt no pain. Tasted no blood. And that screaming, it'd gone too.

"Hello? It's... It's Kathy. I moved in late. I heard something in there. So, um... I hope I'm not talkin' to myself."

Ellicia unlocked the door and opened it right up. Kathy, of course. A Texan girl who was supposed to be getting here midway through first week. Ellicia had chatted to her over Messenger before she'd got here. She'd even told her she wasn't going out tonight 'cause she wasn't feeling it. Damn. She'd forgotten. Totally forgotten.

She opened up the door and saw Kathy standing there, smile on her face.

That smile soon dropped when she saw Ellicia, though. "Sorry. I... Are you okay?"

"Hey, Kathy. Nice—nice to meet."

"You too. Hey, Ellicia, you... you look pretty sick."

"Oh, just the flu, you know?"

"Caught it early?"

"Something like that."

Kathy nodded and attempted a smile. But she didn't look convinced by Ellicia's insisting she was okay. "Anyway. I, um. Just thought I'd check in. Say hi. I'd better go get unpacked."

"Right," Ellicia said. "Flight okay?"

"Delayed. As usual."

"As usual."

Kathy gave another one of those uncertain smiles, like she was holding back from saying something. "I'm, um. I'm in. If you need anythin'."

"Right," Ellicia said, smiling. "I appreciate that."

Kathy started walking away.

Then she stopped and looked back.

"You sure you're okay?"

Ellicia gave a thumbs up and immediately felt like an idiot. Who gave thumbs ups anymore? "A-OK." A-OK? Who the hell said A-OK anymore?

"Well, like I say. You know where I am if you need me."

Kathy walked away.

Ellicia watched her walk down the corridor. Kathy looked back a couple times, shot that uncertain smile in her direction.

When Kathy had gone into her room, Ellicia locked up, turned around and headed for her bed.

She didn't feel particularly sick anymore. Just weird. Like the echoes of that cry she'd heard splitting through her skull were still reverberating. Like she... wasn't totally here, somehow.

She headed over to her window again. Looked out at the city lights, at the stars and the moon above. She thought about Kyle. Wherever he was, she hoped he was okay. Whatever he was doing, she hoped he'd—

The sickening punch in the gut.

The taste of blood, thicker this time.

And worst of all, that screaming.

A screaming that felt like nails on a chalkboard.

Ellicia fell to her knees. She might've smacked her head on her desk. She might've started shouting, having seizures, convoluting. She really didn't have a clue.

'Cause all she could focus on was that scream.

She could hear whose scream it was now.

She recognized the voice.

"Ellicia, no!"

It was Kyle.

And then there was nothing but total silence.

39

I sat back against the wall of rocks and I stared into the darkness.

I had no idea what time of day it was. I didn't know where I was, or how long I'd been here. I was cold. Or... no. Maybe I was warm. I wasn't sure. I was shaking so much that it made me *feel* like I was cold, but perhaps I was completely boiling, but just couldn't recover from the shock.

The shock of what had happened.

When Catalyst cut open my fingertip and dripped a little of my blood into the Failsafe.

I shuddered even more when I recalled the memory. I didn't want to replay it. I didn't want to see what had happened, how it had all played out. I'd seen it once, and once was enough.

I'd tried to stop myself. I'd tried to resist going ahead with what'd happened the second I saw what was happening.

But in the end, my resistance was futile.

The pull of what the Failsafe wanted me to do was just way too strong.

Because that was just how it—and I—had been designed.

I looked up and tried to illuminate my dark surroundings, but I felt too weak, too apathetic, to even care. I listened for sounds, but all I could hear was total silence. Maybe I was still down in the earth at the bottom of a volcano. Maybe Catalyst had left me here until he saw fit to use me and the Failsafe to wipe out the human race.

Or maybe he didn't ever plan on using that Failsafe at all. Maybe it was just a power thing. A control thing.

Whatever. It didn't matter. I was here, and I was stuck down here. He had me, which meant the possibility of his threat was always going to be there.

And he'd been sure to rig the place with total anti-energy to make sure I couldn't teleport out of here or fly my way out of here, no matter what.

And even if I could, I didn't feel strong enough.

Not after what I'd seen happen to Ellicia.

Just the thought of what'd happened made my stomach turn as I saw it playing out again.

At first, he'd cut my fingertip and dropped the blood onto the light of the Failsafe.

Nothing had happened. Not at first. I'd felt slightly light-headed, sure, but I was a wuss with cuts and bruises despite all the bones I'd snapped back into place over the last couple years, so that was hardly surprising.

But then it felt like I'd passed out.

No.

Not passed out. Something had left my body. A bolt of bright energy. I'd seen it leave my chest and I'd followed it. I *became* it. I could see through it.

And when Catalyst told me the Failsafe took down those I cared about mostly first, just by nature of its design, I knew how much trouble I was in.

I'd passed by New York, by Staten Island, and for a split second I'd felt relief because that meant Dad and Avi were okay.

But then I'd seen the Golden Gate bridge, and my stomach —even though I was having some kind of out of body experience —dropped.

Ellicia.

I shook my head and dismissed the thought, the memory. It wasn't good for me. I couldn't keep on thinking back, replaying it in my mind.

It was no use. Not anymore. What was done was done, and I couldn't do a thing to change that. Not a damned thing.

I didn't want to think back. I wanted to occupy myself some other way. The Resistance. The rest of them. Where were they? Did Catalyst still have them prisoner? Could I help them in some way? Could I...

My energy drained, once again.

I'd failed them. I'd fallen into Michael Williamson and Catalyst's trap and I'd allowed myself to be used. So much for responsibility. So much for being a hero. I'd been used as a weapon. A tool.

And the only way I could truly take responsibility was to just give up.

Because Ellicia was gone...

The memory flashed into my head again, strong in all its glory.

This time, I saw myself as that bolt of energy flying through the winding, hilly streets of San Francisco.

I saw Ellicia's apartment up ahead.

I saw her flat.

Her room.

And then I saw her.

She was standing by the door when I saw her. And it was as if time slowed right down. I let out a cry. A deafening cry.

And then I saw her look right at me and fire rose from her body.

Something happened, then. The energy was too strong. Too powerful. I'd blacked out.

But then I'd woken again.

I'd become conscious.

And this time, I'd seen her making her way toward her bed.

I wanted to tell her to stop. To.... Shit, to just do anything but allow me to get to her.

But there was nothing I could do.

I slammed into her back and heard her cry.

And when I did, I cried out too.

I felt the burning pain and tasted blood and heard a chorus of screams.

And then Ellicia had gone still and then, nothingness.

I'd woken up here not long after, in this pit, wherever it was I'd been cast aside. I was weak. I'd tried to escape, but to no avail. I was trapped.

I reached into my pocket and pulled out that little almond necklace Ellicia gave me. I smiled when I rubbed my thumb across it, and tasted tears at the same time. She'd been so kind. So thoughtful. But more than that, she'd given me a chance. A chance to be Kyle Peters. A chance to be me.

And she'd liked me for who I was.

For the first time, she'd made me feel like it was okay to be myself.

I owed her everything for that.

And I'd failed her.

I pressed the almond necklace to my head and I cried. I cried because I thought of the good times we'd had together.

The times drinking milkshakes, the long walks through Manhattan.

And I cried because of the bad times, too. When we'd spent so much time apart during the Battle of the ULTRAs. When she'd left me. Our final goodbye kiss.

Because there was no revisiting that moment, now.

There was no turning back the clock.

Ellicia was gone. And I was...

"You need to grow up and take responsibility."

I heard Ellicia's words as if they were aloud.

"You need to grow up and take responsibility."

And I kept hearing them, over and over. And although they'd been cloudy and fuzzy when she'd first said them, they were making more sense. More and more sense.

Because she was right. I was growing up. I was getting closer to becoming a man. And as much as I hated it, I had responsibilities. I had a duty. Not just to her. Not just to myself. But to everyone. To the Resistance. To the rest of the ULTRAs in this world. And to the people.

I might not like being Glacies. I might not like the idea of being a hero.

But a hero was who I was.

I clenched my fist around that almond necklace she'd made me when she was unaware I was allergic.

I felt my throat tightening before I'd even consumed it.

Because what I was going to do might just be the riskiest thing I'd done.

I had to take a risk because I had to stop Catalyst. I had to take the Failsafe away from him.

I had to end this mess.

I closed my eyes and I pictured myself on a beach, Ellicia by my side, hand in mine.

I felt a tear roll down my cheek as the nerves gave way to pure fear.

"I love you," I mumbled.

Then I stuck the almond necklace in my mouth and waited for the allergic reaction to kick in and kill me.

40

Catalyst stared across the Italian mountains and even though he was miles away from any real civilization, he could still feel the fear in him growing far and wide.

It was a beautiful sunset. He couldn't see it, of course. But he didn't have to. He could feel the light warmth of the sun against his cheeks. He could taste the gradual shift of temperature in the air. The smells were beautiful and fresh. Fall leaves dropping from trees. That cooling scent after a warm fall day.

But it was the *fear* Catalyst felt more than anything.

Especially as the major powers of the world knew what he had now.

Especially now they knew that the Failsafe—not the original, but the one capable of destroying all of humanity—was in his possession.

He looked down and rubbed his hands around the Failsafe. He had grown so used to the feel of it that he knew by now exactly what it looked like. At least, based on his warped idea of what *silver* and black and gray and all colors were.

It was strange, trying to explain imagination to someone

who wasn't blind. People who weren't blind always said it was an impossible task explaining color to a blind person. But they didn't take a moment to consider it was exactly the same in reverse. It was impossible for Catalyst to explain how he interpreted the world.

But he knew one thing for sure.

He was at an advantage. Because he didn't get distracted by the things people with eyes did. He didn't get lured in by television or "man-made wonders" or any of that nonsense.

He just *saw* what was. What his senses offered him.

And he had a greater picture of the world than the average person.

He heard movement drifting toward him and he knew it was one of his ULTRAs. See, he'd found room for expansion since gaining possession of both Glacies and the Failsafe. He didn't intend to use the Failsafe. Not just yet, anyway. Not until he absolutely had to. It was a ransom device more than anything. A way of getting what he wanted, when he wanted. The ultimate bargaining chip.

But he would use it eventually. That was the difference between him and the average businessman or woman that might have this Failsafe in their possession. The average businessperson would sell it off to the highest bidder. Use it as a power thing.

Catalyst, on the other hand, wasn't going to give the Failsafe away to anyone. He wasn't going to sell it to anyone.

He was going to use it to get what he wanted.

And then he was going to use it to get rid of what he didn't want.

What did he want?

Power.

Total, unobstructed power.

He knew it wouldn't be easy. He knew getting the world's

governments to give up even a fraction of their power wasn't going to be easy.

But when they did give that power up, Catalyst would make them beg. He'd make them beg for something back. He'd put the governments through absolute hell and get them on their knees until they begged him to just give up his demands, hand over the Failsafe, and hand over Glacies.

But Catalyst was never going to give in to their demands.

In fact, he was only going to make them give up their power for his own satisfaction. Just to watch them descend into fear, piece by piece.

Then he was going to take everything away from them.

Just for fun.

He looked down at the gaping volcano below. Glacies was down there, way down there. He was weak, though. Just triggering the Failsafe on a minor level had enough energy to take it out of him completely.

Besides, he'd made Glacies take out someone closest to him.

That wasn't exactly going to motivate Glacies.

He had plans for Glacies. Plans to reveal to the people of the world where he stood in the pecking order now. Where Catalyst stood in the pecking order.

And where humanity stood in the pecking order.

His smile turned as he imagined the faces of the people—people who'd spent a lifetime treading him down, kicking him into the dirt, messing around and experimenting with him—realizing they weren't at the top of the food chain again. In fact, they were way below the top of the food chain. They were the lowest of the low.

He'd enjoy watching them writhe in pain and fear.

Then, naturally, he'd take it all away.

He'd have plenty of time to enjoy with humanity. Plenty of time.

But for now, he had someone else in his possession.

He drifted down toward the volcano, through the gap where the lava had raised up out of not long ago. The further he descended, the colder he got. He imagined Glacies down there, freezing, suffering from guilt. And you know, Catalyst actually felt a twinge of pity, just for a moment. 'Cause he didn't have anything *personal* against Glacies. Sure, he'd tried to stand against him. He'd acted like a good cop, like he was the world police or something. He'd tried to make people and ULTRAs do what he wanted them to do. And for that reason, he was an irritant. A pest.

But Glacies had never done anything personal to hurt Catalyst. No more than the average person, anyway.

Yet it was just what he represented that made Catalyst's skin crawl.

Glacies was the most powerful ULTRA. He was the spawn of Orion. Orion represented a major beginning of the "Hero" experiment. Or at least, the beginning in the eyes of the public, after Alpha and all the others.

The first real Hero.

He represented the Frankenstein's monster that Catalyst was.

The contorted, blind beast that he'd been turned into.

He tried not to think about the time before his blindness and his abilities, which made him feel sick. Not often.

But as he got closer to Glacies, he saw a flash of the past in his mind.

He saw the government troops raiding his house.

Making his mom, his dad, all of them sit on their knees.

And as much as they told him he'd forget, that his mind and memories would be wiped, he remembered.

He remembered them killing his mom and dad.

He remembered them taking him away. Sticking pins and needles and blades and everything into him.

He remembered them taking his eyes out.

All he forgot was what it was ever like to have seen.

Every little piece of agony that he was supposed to have forgotten came flying back, and all that memory did was make him hate Glacies, for standing up for the whims of the government and the whims of the evil people who'd done this to him.

He reached the point where he was keeping Glacies. He tried to hear his breathing, to feel the warmth in the air from his breaths.

But there was nothing.

Nothing but coughing.

Nothing but choking.

And then... just nothing.

Catalyst tensed his jaw and flew down to where he knew Glacies was. Something was wrong. Terribly wrong. Something had happened. Something had gone wrong.

But how?

He was supposed to be prisoner.

He was supposed to be his captive.

He was supposed to be safe...

When Catalyst landed in front of Glacies, he knew from the temperature in the air and the echoes of what had happened that something was terribly wrong.

He put a hand on Glacies' chest.

He was still.

Totally still.

His heart was slowing to a standstill.

And he'd stopped breathing.

41

I felt my throat tightening and I saw myself when I was a little kid again.

I was in some kind of park. Central Park, I think. It was the middle of summer, and the day was stifling hot. I'd been moaning for an ice cream all morning, making Mom and Dad's days hell. Cassie was out with some friends, and in truth, I was missing her. I preferred it when she was here. We had more fun.

But she wasn't. And I was in a terrible mood.

Anyway, I'd finally seen an ice cream stall that had the kind of ice cream I wanted. Not like the other trashy ice cream stalls. The big ones with two cones. I especially liked the look of those ones that the big man behind the counter was coating in chocolate.

And after he coated it in chocolate, which magically went hard again right away, he sprinkled some little nuts on it.

I licked my lips. That was the ice cream I wanted. Cassie might not be here and it might not be as fun without Cassie, but she was gonna wish she was here when she saw which ice cream I'd got. I was gonna make her so jealous.

"Mom?"

Mom shook her head. Now the memory played through my mind, I noticed extra details. The sweat on her forehead. The twitching smile at the corner of her lips, like she'd had enough of my demands for the day. Dad was by her side, and he'd barely spoken to me since I started whining. He had a good way of doing that, which annoyed young me, and which young me didn't really understand at the time. But when Mom didn't answer, I looked at him.

"Dad?"

He glanced around at me, thin smile on his face. "What's up?"

I lifted my finger, glad I'd got his attention more than anything, and pointed over toward the ice cream stall. "That one."

Dad lifted a finger too and followed where I was pointed. "Oh, that one?"

I smiled. "Yeah. Yeah, that one."

Dad lowered his hand. "Well, you said that about the last one."

"No, but this one I really want—"

"Well you forgot the magic word."

My cheeks started flushing. "Dad I just want an—"

"You want an ice cream? You can learn some manners. Come on. Let's get to the museum before it closes."

I couldn't believe Dad had just outright rejected me. Again, I didn't totally interpret it like that at the time. More just confusion. Dad had started listening to me, actually looked at the ice cream stall, and then he'd turned around and told Mom to carry on.

So I did what any little kid, slightly overheated, a little dehydrated, and very tired, did.

I dug my heels into the ground and let out a wail.

I saw Mom roll her eyes. Saw Dad sigh, shake his head.

"Kyle," Mom said, reaching for my hand.

"I want an ice cream!"

"You definitely are *not* getting an ice cream anymore," Dad grumbled. "Not with this behavior."

"I hate you!"

"Right," Dad said, taking my other hand. "That's it."

When Mom and Dad both grabbed my hands, pulling me away, I wasn't sure what possessed me to act how I did. I'd seen people playing dead before, acting like something bad happened to them. I'd seen it on TV and I'd seen Cassie do it a few times when she was playing with friends.

So what did I think was a good idea right now?

I rolled my eyes back, closed them, and let all my muscles go weak.

For a moment, Mom and Dad dragged me along. I felt my knees scraping against the ground.

Then I sensed the confusion. Felt them slowing down. Heard the panic.

And that's when I knew I'd had my big break.

I enjoyed it for a few seconds. Enjoyed that cruel worry I was causing them. Enjoyed the shouts all around calling for help. I got a bit scared when someone mentioned calling the ambulance, so I figured that was a good chance to open my eyes.

When I came round, it was like the day had been reset. I saw Mom smiling at me, stroking my head. Dad... well, he wasn't exactly showing emotion, per se. But he wasn't shouting at me, so that was some kind of progress I figured.

"Oh, Kyle," Mom said, wrapping her arms around me. "You're okay. You—you just had a little fall, that's all. Just fainted. Just for a second."

I soaked up the attention as Mom called me a brave boy and people passed by smiling at me.

I was plotting how I was going to approach the ice cream question when I realized I didn't even have to.

The ice cream man was walking to me, chocolate and almond covered ice cream in hand.

He stuck it out. "Figure you'll wanna get your blood sugar back up. This one's on me."

I looked at Mom and Dad for approval. And finally, they let me take my ice cream.

The first bite was delicious. The crispness of the thick layer of chocolate. The coldness of the ice cream.

It was the crunch of the almonds where things started to take a turn.

When I felt my throat tightening.

When I saw colors in my eyes.

When everything around me went blurry.

I might've fake-fainted just minutes before. But now, I was really fainting. For the first time in my life.

The last thing I knew before getting to the hospital was Mom carrying me in her arms.

I felt that again, right now. I felt her carrying me some-where, fast. I could *feel* her panic. Feel her pain. And I wanted to make it better. I wanted to...

My eyes opened a little and I realized it wasn't Mom carrying me at all. It couldn't be Mom carrying me, because Mom was gone.

There was only one person carrying me right now.

And I didn't want to be in their arms.

I squeezed my fingers together. They were numb and shak-ing. I could barely breathe.

But I had to.

Because I was in Catalyst's arms.

Which meant my plan had worked.

Now I just had to do the hard part.

As weak as I was after the Failsafe incident, as unmotivated as I was after what had happened to Ellicia, and as on death's door as I was from the allergic reaction, I knew I couldn't just give up.

It was my responsibility to fight.

It was my responsibility to be a Hero.

It was my responsibility to be Glacies.

Even if it killed me.

My eyes opened some more.

I pushed. Pushed to spark my powers, while staying as stealthy as I could.

I could do this if I believed.

I could do this if I really tried.

I was weak. Dizzy. Hazy. And I was going to pass out again if I wasn't careful.

But screw it.

I wasn't here to be careful.

I was here to save the world.

I clenched my teeth together and one final time, as a tear rolled down my cheek, I pictured Ellicia and all the love I felt for her, all the pain I'd felt at losing her.

Then I felt power surge from my chest.

For a split second, although Catalyst couldn't see, I swore he looked down at me, like he knew something was happening.

"Unlucky," I said.

Then I grabbed the sides of his head and I teleported us away from here.

When we re-appeared, the snow was heavy from above and thick below.

The ice was biting.

But I was standing.

I was covered in ice.

We were on my territory now.

42

I wasn't totally back to full strength. I could still feel the darned almond allergy eating away at me inside.

But I was on my feet.

Catalyst was on his ass.

And we were in the middle of Antarctica.

So it looked to me like I had the advantage again.

It was dark, but for a glimmer of light that peeked over the horizon. Naturally, it was freezing. The snow underfoot was thick and it fell heavily from above. If I wasn't Glacies—icy by nature—I'd probably have contracted hypothermia already.

I could tell from the way that Catalyst was lying there, shaking and gasping for air, his breath freezing on his face the second he let it go, that I was at a good advantage right now.

I walked toward him, eager to get done what I had to get done. Because it was simple, now. I saw it clearly.

The Failsafe couldn't be trusted in the hands of anybody.

As long as the Failsafe was in existence, humanity would be at risk.

And I was a key part to the threat of that Failsafe.

Without *me,* there was no threat.

I stepped over Catalyst and grabbed his neck with an icy hand.

I tensed and lifted him up, putting all my strength and power into raising him into the air. His shaking body fell flimsily below. He made a few half-hearted punches and kicks, but I could tell he was clearly in deep shock with the cold.

And I was going to make him a whole lot colder.

"You won't kill me," I said. "Because you need me to activate that Failsafe. You need me to be powerful. So you can try locking me away. You can try pinning me down with a million anti-energy bolts. You can try any damned thing. But as long as I'm alive, I'm never going to give up who I am."

I tightened my grip around his neck and felt his skin go hard as the ice froze him.

"I am Glacies. I am a Hero. That's just who I am."

I kept on holding tight as the energy drifted from Catalyst's body. I didn't like what I was doing. But I still didn't feel recharged enough to open another wormhole and send him flying through it, not after opening the last one so recently.

Besides, I was done with wormholes. I was through with them.

People like Catalyst never gave up.

So it was time to send out a message.

More of Catalyst's skin went cold and hard. He reached out a hand, gently put it on the back of mine. He'd stopped shaking, and his heart was beating very, very slowly. He was almost down. Almost completely out.

"Never..."

I barely heard his voice. "What did you say?"

"Never... give up."

I didn't understand what Catalyst said until I felt a thumping blast right in the center of my chest.

I went flying back. I hit the snow with force, barging

through it and winding myself in the process. I tried to shuffle out of this mess, tried to stand, when I felt another punch in my chest and went further down into the snow.

Catalyst was above me.

Shaking, but above me.

He was rabid with anger.

"You might say you'll never give up," he said, before cracking a head-splitting punch right across my temple. "But neither will I. I'll never give up what I want, either."

Another punch cracked against my head, knocking back what energy I'd recharged.

I felt anger. I felt pain.

I scrambled to feel and embrace love before—

Another punch.

Borderline unconsciousness.

My throat was closing up again as my resistance to the allergy, which was taking everything out of me, faded.

Catalyst picked me up then, and threw me out of this hole of snow we were in.

I landed right at the side of an icy lake. I heard cracking all around me with the force of my fall. The ice was thick, but I knew it'd only take one tap from either of us ULTRAs to split it open.

Catalyst appeared above me. I barely saw him through my blurred, swollen eyes. I'd used the last of my energy, and now all of it was focused on holding off that allergy, keeping it from killing me.

I didn't have any more energy left.

But I wasn't sure I needed it.

Catalyst lifted the Failsafe out of his pocket. He opened it, and the light beamed from it.

Then in his other hand, he lifted a long, sharp knife.

"Any final words?" he asked, teeth chattering, lowering the

knife and the Failsafe toward me.

I had lots of final words. Things I wanted to say. Things I *needed* to say.

But in the end, I just found myself smiling and laughing.

"I hope you're a good swimmer."

Catalyst's face twitched.

He shuffled back, right off the ice, so I couldn't send him falling under it.

But he didn't realize that he'd just done exactly what I'd wanted.

Given me some time.

I closed my eyes. Or they closed over, I wasn't sure which.

I let my throat swell up to the point I couldn't breathe.

I thought of Dad. I thought of Cassie. I thought of Damon. Avi. Ellicia.

Mom.

And then I lifted a fist, threw all the love and the pain into it, and slammed it against the ice.

I heard the ice crack around me.

"No!" Catalyst shouted.

And for a moment, I thought he was going to get to me.

Then I fell.

Total freezing cold water covered me.

It slipped into my nostrils.

Poured into my lungs.

And as I sank down into the water, I thought I saw a light above.

And that light was in the shape of my mom.

She held out her hand, smiling.

"Come on, now, Kyle. Come on."

I reached my hand up and grabbed onto her.

Everything went cold, dark, and silent.

But I'd never felt warmer in my entire life.

43

Catalyst listened to the water rippling against the cracked ice and couldn't quite believe what he'd just witnessed.

The snow had eased. He was still freezing, totally freezing, but somehow he felt numb to it. Perhaps it was hypothermia kicking in. Or maybe he was just growing hardened to it.

Whatever it was, he couldn't quite get his head around what had happened.

Kyle had lay back on the ice. He'd punched the ice hard with his powers.

And then he'd fallen down into the water.

Catalyst swallowed a dry lump in his throat. He was sure Kyle wasn't strong enough to use his powers anymore. He'd been having an allergic reaction, and it was clear to Catalyst that he was using his abilities to stave that reaction off.

But Catalyst had felt the shift in the air.

He'd felt the change of power from Kyle.

He'd let that allergy take over his body and he'd sacrificed himself.

All so Catalyst could never use the Failsafe.

He felt a creeping sensation in his chest. The sides of his mouth started to twitch. Because the more he perched here, in total disbelief, the more he realized the ramifications of what had just unfolded.

Kyle had sacrificed himself so that Catalyst could never use the Failsafe. So that *nobody* could ever use the Failsafe.

Which rendered Catalyst powerless.

Well. Not totally powerless. He was strong. Stronger than perhaps anyone, now that Glacies was...

No. He couldn't accept Glacies was gone.

He had to do something about it.

Because he was strong. No doubt about that.

But strong was no good. Strong wasn't what he wanted to be.

He wanted to have total control.

Without Glacies to make the Failsafe complete and allow him to rule over the humans using fear, before purging them, one by one, he was just another ULTRA.

He held his breath and walked across the ice. It had frozen over almost immediately, thick and solid.

With every step Catalyst took, he increased the power with which he lowered his feet. He kept on increasing that power, using his abilities, until he heard the first crack in the ice.

And when he did, he added a little more power, kept on going, until there was a hole in the ice.

A hole that he had to go down into if he wanted to stand any chance of finding Glacies and saving him before he died.

Or at least using him while the final bit of life was still left.

Catalyst perched closer toward the opening. He could feel how cold the water was even when he wasn't in contact. When he was younger, he'd gone snorkeling in the Thingvellir National Park in Iceland, between the tectonic plates. It'd been an amazing experience, but it'd been a cold experience. And it wasn't one he was keen to replicate.

He dipped his little finger in the water and immediately jolted it back with the bitter, painful cold.

He bit his lip. No way. No way was he climbing in that water. It was insane. It'd kill him. Finish him off.

Maybe that's what he had to do, anyway. After all, Kyle had proven himself willing to sacrifice himself for a cause. Maybe if Catalyst could find Kyle, he could activate the Failsafe and die in the process.

It would be a shame to miss the fireworks as humanity collapsed. A great shame.

But at least his final act would be the most devastating, important act in the history of the planet.

At least his final act would be one of kindness toward the world.

He took a few deep breaths, still unable to believe he was actually considering doing this.

But it was his responsibility to do this.

It was his legacy to do this.

He leaned his head back and dulled his senses, eased his mind.

He held his breath.

Activated his strength, so at least he'd be able to fly down into that water and slam into the depths, getting it done with as quickly as possible.

Then he held a foot over the icy water and plunged into it.

It was even colder than he'd expected.

The pain was sudden. He felt like he was being stabbed all over. He tried to hold his breath, but he couldn't help opening his mouth, screaming in silence.

He felt like he was waking up again after a long, dreamless

sleep. He lost all sense of what he was doing, of why he was down here in the water.

Then it came flooding back into his mind.

The urgency.

Find Kyle.

Activate the Failsafe.

Do what you have to do.

He drifted further down into the water. He knew he didn't have long left. He had to get this done with, and he had to get it done with fast.

He felt the water temperature for a sign of warmth. Kyle would be cold, sure, but anything would seem like lava compared to the surrounding water.

He kept on descending down. And the more he sank, the less his thoughts made sense. The more they became abstract, not adding up.

And the more he needed to breathe.

He was about to turn around and give up when he felt a mass of warmth right ahead of him.

He reached out. Grabbed it.

When he felt the object, he knew right away what it was.

Who it was.

Kyle.

He pulled out the Failsafe, unable to stop his lips from opening. The icy cold trickled into his lungs, almost finishing him off right here.

But he was almost there.

Almost done.

Then he grabbed the knife. Placed it against Kyle's chest.

His heart was still beating, very slowly.

He still had time to do this.

He still had time to finish his life's goal.

He sensed his family in his mind. Heard his mother's voice. Felt her soft hair.

Then he pulled back the knife.

For a split second, something strange happened.

Something very strange.

Catalyst couldn't describe the sensation. Kind of like dreaming, only way more detailed, way more lucid.

It was when he saw the person beneath him, floating away, that he realized he was *seeing* again.

He was seeing, all over again.

Only he didn't feel joyous or relieved for long.

Not when he saw that Kyle's eyes were wide open, too.

And he was holding onto Catalyst's arm.

He smiled at Catalyst.

Then something sparked across his body.

Something perfect.

Something blue.

Electr—

Catalyst didn't have any more thoughts after that.

He just felt a million knives pierce through his body.

He felt his grip on the Failsafe slip. And as much as he wanted to go after it, he couldn't. He was trapped. He was paralyzed.

Kyle Peters held onto Catalyst for ten long, grueling seconds, the electricity pouring from his arms and shocking the pair of them.

After those ten seconds passed, Catalyst was still.

Kyle was still.

They sunk down into the depths of the water, right below Antarctica, as the opening above froze over.

The Failsafe drifted even further beneath them.

Both of them were silent.

44

Three weeks later

DAMON RACED down the hospital corridor, eager not to be late for this.

It was snowing like mad outside. Freak weather for the last couple days. Hailstone. Snow. Rain. Wind. Everything. You hate it, name it, it's probably happened.

And sure, Damon was drenched. Completely drenched, head to toe.

But he'd come out in the rain and the storm, despite all the weather warnings, over to the hospital because he couldn't miss what was waiting for him.

Who was waiting for him.

Alive.

He felt his stomach tingle as he raced through the main entrance area to the corridor leading to the wards. He dodged a woman holding a clipboard, then ended up stuck behind two old people walking crazy slow. He thought about sparking up his electricity, blasting them out of the way. Cruel to be kind, sorta thing.

In the end, they took a left, and his road to the ward he had to get to was clear all over again.

He was so, so close.

He ran further down the corridor. His trainers squeaked in contact with the floor with every step. They were wet through. Behind, he heard someone calling out to him, telling him to stop because he was creating a hazard.

Screw the hazard. He'd let someone else deal with it.

Because his friend was still alive.

He'd found out the news fifteen minutes ago and the moment he heard it, he'd been right down here. He hadn't told his parents where he was heading. Hadn't told Avi, or anyone.

He would tell them. He'd tell them in time. But right now, his friend needed someone beside them. Someone to... Well. Someone there for them.

Because his friend was on their own now.

He held back the tears when he thought about the loss. The loss he'd suffered. The loss all of them had suffered. And he knew he needed to make sure he was the rock for the person that was still living.

After all, it's what his friend would've wanted.

He'd got out of Vesuvius. As had the rest of the Resistance. Vortex had struggled. There was something wrong with her. Something making her weaker that she couldn't explain. And Roadrunner, too. Something suspicious about her. She'd seemed far too eager to get back to... to... well, wherever it was she wanted to get back to.

But anyway. They'd searched for Kyle, tried to find him everywhere, but to no avail. And then the news broke...

No. The news was too painful to think about.

He went to take a right turn when he slipped over and smacked his head against the floor.

He rubbed his head, feeling dizzy and sick. His ankle hurt, and he knew he should probably see someone about it. But hey. He'd get the chance to do that. He was in the right place.

But he couldn't waste any more time.

He got up, still rubbing the back of his head. He could feel a little blood, so he'd definitely have to get it checked out.

Still, he turned the corner, headed into Ward 34, and began his search.

He hurried down the ward, looking at each and every bed. He didn't want to miss the bed he was looking for. He didn't want to accidentally walk by.

But the further he got down the corridor, the more Damon wondered if he'd perhaps got the wrong ward. Maybe he'd made a mistake, heard the number wrong, or something. It was just all old people in here. Smelly old people, coughing and spluttering, looking at him through wide eyes in their pale, bony skulls.

He was about to give up and search another ward when he saw them.

They were sitting upright in the bed like they were just kicking back at home, watching Netflix.

But as Damon got closer, he saw they didn't look well. Not as fresh-faced as they usually did. Not as much color in their cheeks.

But they were alive.

That was the main thing.

They were alive.

They turned around and looked right at Damon.

"Damon?"

Damon's smile tugged at the corners of his mouth, pulling it right up his face. "Ellicia," he said.

He walked over to Ellicia's bedside and without any regard

for what kind of state Ellicia might be in, he hugged her. She hugged him back, holding him tight.

"We thought you were gone," he said.

"Well, me too. But I'm still here. I'm still here."

Damon felt his eyes clouding over, then. He wondered if she knew. Really, he should be the one to tell her. The one to break the news.

He pulled away from Ellicia and looked her right in her eyes, as difficult as that was. "Ellicia, there's something I need to—"

"I know," she said.

Damon frowned. "Huh?"

Ellicia smiled. "I know. About Kyle. About what happened to him." She pointed up at the screen at the end of her bed. Rolling news coverage about the disappearance of Glacies, about how he was believed to be dead, based on seismic activity and all that weirdness.

But Ellicia didn't seem particularly... bothered. If anything, she seemed kind of content.

"How come you're... you're so chilled. About it all?"

Ellicia looked around at Damon and her smile widened. "Because I don't think he's gone."

Damon swallowed a lump in his throat. "I... The news say—"

"The news say a lot of things. But they don't know him like we do, Damon. They don't know how strong he is. What he's capable of."

She turned back to the screen, where two panelists were discussing the "death of Glacies," and she turned the television off.

"He visited me," Ellicia said.

Damon frowned. He almost slipped again. "What... How—"

"About a week ago. I felt him next to me. Felt his cold hand holding mine. He told me to be strong. That everything was going to be okay." She wiped away a tear. "And it is now. Right?"

"But you've been in a coma for three weeks."

"Maybe so. But I didn't have any dreams in that coma. I just knew Kyle was beside me at one point. And hey. We're still here, right? So whatever happened, whoever Kyle was fighting, he has to have won."

Damon knew Ellicia was right. Catalyst was gone. His body had been found in the water between Argentina and Antarctica by a touring cruise. That's what started the search for Kyle across Antarctica.

And they'd eventually found traces of his blood, deep under the ice.

Then, the search had ended.

"Just because he's won doesn't mean he's still here," Damon said.

"Thought you were here to cheer me up?"

"Sorry. I—"

"It's okay. It's okay. I just... I don't want to believe he's still here. I don't have to believe it. I just do. Don't you?"

Damon didn't want to upset Ellicia by telling her what he thought.

So instead, he just leaned over and hugged her again.

"Wherever he is, he saved everyone," he said. "He saved everyone all over again."

"Because he's a hero," Ellicia said. "And he stepped up. Just like he knew he had to all along."

Damon sighed, and nodded. He looked over at the window outside the hospital. "He is a hero. And he always will be."

He stared out of the window at the falling snow, as the sky darkened, and he held on to Ellicia, his friend.

Then he closed his eyes and the pair of them cried.

THE SNOW CONTINUED to fall outside the window.

Damon and Ellicia kept on hugging.

They didn't see the speck of frost creep up the glass, then disappear.

Like it'd been brushed by magic.

Or by fingertips...

45

I opened my eyes and gasped for air.

I saw darkness. Darkness all around me. Darkness everywhere.

I tried to squint but I couldn't see a thing.

All the while I kept on gasping.

Kept on spluttering.

I wasn't sure where I was. When I was. *Who* I was wasn't even particularly clear.

All I knew was that I should be dead.

Wherever I was, and whenever I was, I should be—

"Kyle?"

Kyle. Yes. That was my name. Kyle Peters. Staten Island. Went to high school at...

"Or should we say, 'Glacies?'"

Another voice in the darkness. This one was different. Deeper. And yet like the other one, it was strangely familiar.

And like the other one, it triggered a whole barrage of memories.

I was Kyle Peters.

I was Glacies. Hero. ULTRA.

I'd just defeated Catalyst.

I'd sacrificed myself to make sure the Failsafe could never hurt anyone.

And now I was...

Well, where was I now?

What was I now?

"Can he see us?"

"He'll see us when he's ready."

I tried to open my mouth and speak but my jaw ached so much and my throat was raw. I was disoriented by the darkness. It felt like I was floating. Like there was no up, no down, no direction in any way.

Then I saw a sudden piercing light right ahead of me.

I covered my eyes. The light was painful. And as much as I had no idea how long I'd been out cold, I felt like it'd been a long time. A very long time. It had to have been.

But I saw the light fading. And in that light, I could see a figure. A silhouette. Someone I recognized. Someone I'd seen before. Someone I'd...

Then I saw another.

Another silhouette, right by the side of that familiar figure.

And as they got closer, I grew more and more convinced that I was dead.

As they drifted closer, I grew more certain that they weren't real. That this was some kind of hallucination.

But they kept on getting closer.

And soon enough, they were close enough for me to make out clearly.

"Kyle," the voice on the left said. "Good to see you again. Bro."

I blinked a few times, and I saw exactly who it was.

Daniel Peters. Nycto. My brother.

And by his side...

Orion.

My biological father.

"How..." I started, unable to spit the words out. "How did—"

"There's a time and a place for how and why," another voice said.

This voice came from behind me. And when I heard it, it made my arms shiver all over.

Because I recognized that voice.

I recognized it clearly.

I turned around and I saw Saint floating toward me.

I went to activate my abilities but nothing happened. I tried to fly at Saint, but I just went wobbling past him, bouncing against the walls of darkness.

When I looked back, reorienting myself, I saw that he was by Daniel and Orion's side.

"Don't worry about me," Saint said. "I am the least of your worries right now."

"He's telling the truth," Orion said.

Daniel shrugged. "What he said."

I couldn't believe what I was looking at. What I was hearing. "This can't be real. This can't be real."

"It is real," Saint said.

He hovered up so he was directly opposite me.

"You don't have to worry about me right now because there's a greater threat. A far, far greater threat, getting closer and closer as we speak."

"What threat? What—what is this?"

"The apocalypse is coming, Kyle. And it's approaching fast."

"What's going on?"

"Do you want to see?" Saint asked.

I looked past Saint. Down at Daniel, at Orion. For some sort of sign that this must be a trap. That this wasn't what it looked like.

But in the end, I found myself looking back at Saint, intrigued by what he was asking.

"Yes," I said.

A smile crept across Saint's scarred mouth. "Good," he said. "Then I'll show you."

He hovered out of the way.

And then something started happening.

Together, between him, Daniel and Orion, it felt like the darkness was peeling away. Like the sky or whatever was around us was just falling apart like old wallpaper.

And when they'd pulled all that old wallpaper away, I saw what was behind it.

Exactly what was behind it.

"Now, do you understand?" Saint asked.

I hovered alongside Saint, Orion, and Daniel, and I stared up into the sky.

I stared up at what was coming. I was speechless. All I could manage was: "What... what is...?"

Saint put a hand on my back. And it said a lot about how stunned I was that I didn't even flinch upon contact by my greatest foe. "That, my boy, is the apocalypse. And it's coming right for us. For everyone."

WANT MORE FROM MATT BLAKE?

The sixth book in The Last Hero series, Fall of the ULTRAs, is now available to buy.

If you want to be notified when Matt Blake's next novel in The Last Hero series is released, please sign up for the mailing list by going to: http://mattblakeauthor.com/newsletter Your email address will never be shared and you can unsubscribe at any time.

Word-of-mouth and reviews are crucial to any author's success. If you enjoyed this book, please leave a review. Even just a couple of lines sharing your thoughts on the story would be a fantastic help for other readers.

mattblakeauthor.com
mattblake@mattblakeauthor.com

Made in the USA
Coppell, TX
09 November 2021

65461672R00129